Carlene

A Love Story

Tayo Akiwumi

Order this book online at www.trafford.com/07-2757
or email orders@trafford.com

Most Trafford titles are also available at major online book retailers.

Note for Librarians: A cataloguing record for this book is available from Library and Archives Canada at www.collectionscanada.ca/amicus/index-e.html

ISBN: 978-1-4251-6075-3

We at Trafford believe that it is the responsibility of us all, as both individuals and corporations, to make choices that are environmentally and socially sound. You, in turn, are supporting this responsible conduct each time you purchase a Trafford book, or make use of our publishing services. To find out how you are helping, please visit www.trafford.com/responsiblepublishing.html

Our mission is to efficiently provide the world's finest, most comprehensive book publishing service, enabling every author to experience success. To find out how to publish your book, your way, and have it available worldwide, visit us online at www.trafford.com/10510

www.trafford.com

North America & international
toll-free: 1 888 232 4444 (USA & Canada)
phone: 250 383 6864 • fax: 250 383 6804 • email: info@trafford.com

The United Kingdom & Europe
phone: +44 (0)1865 722 113 • local rate: 0845 230 9601
facsimile: +44 (0)1865 722 868 • email: info.uk@trafford.com

10 9 8 7 6 5 4 3 2

About the author

An international marketer by profession, Tayo Akiwumi has a particular love for Far-East Asia and has spent many years travelling in that region. Raised in London, England he has since travelled to over 40 countries across the globe and has lived in Africa, Europe, Middle-East and Asia including Dubai and Bangkok.

'Carlene - A Love Story' is Tayo Akiwumi's first novel.

For my father (R.I.P.), and mother, Bolaji and Yemisi Akiwumi, for their sacrifices, love and firm guidance.

For the rest of my family: for their constant love.

Deep thanks to friends and colleagues like Sonoyo, Jiang Yan and Kayleigh Chung who spent many hours helping to comb through 'Carlene' and giving feedback that helped shape a better novel.

1

It was yet another stifling day in Lagos. The hustle and the bustle of street vendors ring through the air, intermingling with the incessant blare of car horns, childishly demanding attention. Child hawkers carry trays of food, matches, cigarettes, whatever they could, on their head. Many were not much older than me. They were barely 10 years of age.

I knew the pavement was hot from the pounding by the sun yet my feet sent no sensation of pain as I walked briskly, over the busy bridge that connects Lagos Island to the mainland. I walked barefoot, no different to some of my peers and the grownups I passed on my journey, my adventure. I was determined not to return. By rights, and by my judgment, I should never even have had to go through this in the first place.

I couldn't blame my mother for having left me in the care of her half-sister and left my brother and sister with my paternal grand-mother. These were probably the logical options she and my father had before she embarked on her own journey and adventure, to a new world, and for her, a new land called Great Britain. Not much more than two years before her departure, my father had left to study there, two years later my mother joined him.

How was she to know they had left their eldest child in the care of an uncaring woman albeit a close relative.

My uncle was well-to-do and had a large family with 5 children that I was aware of anyway. There were four boys and a girl, only the girl was younger than me, the others were older although one was just a year or so older.

For two long years, I lived with my aunt's family, not as a relative born to her half-sister but rather more as an extension of the domestic staff for her home.

I ran the daily errands I was assigned and shared the chores with the housemaid. A twin set of scars close to the inside of my right wrist is a life-long reminder of one of these errands. On a stormy, rainy day, whilst returning from buying cooked food from street vendors for an older cousin, I slipped and fell. The plates I carried crashed to the ground and I landed on some broken pieces, cutting my wrist. The cuts only just missed a major vein in my wrist.

Worse was to come.

***

During the years I was with my aunt, I rarely attended school; I was the protégé of the cousin closest to my age, Rotimi. We would spend our bus allowance on food and whatnots and walk to school. Sometimes we would go to school then 'hop-off' or simply not go to school at all and head off in the direction of Bar Beach. There on the beach, we would just hang out. Watch people, skip stones in the water, every now and then we would catch catfish and take them back to school to sell or just use them to show off to our peers.

It was during one of these fish-napping escapades that I lost my grip as I tried to lower myself along a slimy, algae covered wall of an open gutter which led to the sea.

It was an easy place to catch small fish such as catfish that were trapped in the gutter. I fell, landing on my right knee, shattering the joint and the knee bone cut through the flesh, protruding by an inch and half. Needless to say, I was in excruciating pain as I lay at the bottom of the gutter, knee bleeding profusely and writhing in never-ending, pulses of pain.

With the help of my shocked and worried cousin, somehow I managed to clamber up the same slimy walls that had aided my fall unable to bare the slightest pressure on my right leg. How we made it to the hospital without money was a minor miracle.

My aunt was contacted by the hospital staff and strangely all I recollect is a vision of my grandmother visiting me during my knee operation, no one else.

Years later, I would look on this as a major turning point in my early life. There's nothing quite like pain to help sharpen a person's focus on the important issues.

My knee seemed to have healed quite well and only a slight tingling sensation remained whenever I over-exerted it.

***

Walking through the ramshackle gate leading the way to my granny's colonial style home, I wondered at how it was that I was the one chosen to live with my inattentive aunty.

Mammy-nurse was the first person I saw, as she hobbled energetically across the front yard.

She expressed shock, naturally, at the sight of the child she had partly nursed along with my siblings in this very home. She fussed of course, as to what I was doing here and how had I got here and what seemed like a zillion other questions. The one that stood out was "have you had something to eat child?"

My brother, sister and cousin were still at school that day and my granny had gone to the market with the driver and houseboy.

I played in the back garden first, climbing the guava tree until I could see over the wall into the massive gardens of the cinema complex next door which also belonged to my family. It had all been one incredible sized estate in a prime location decades before but had been partitioned to provide space for a cinema complex to be built and rented out. In those days, cowboy western and improbable South Asian movies were the most popular at the cinema.

Guava had always been one of my favourite fruits and right next to the two guava trees was a staggered row of shorter trees bearing paw-paw fruits which am also still very partial to. I chased lizards along the rough cement wall bordering the left side of the house until they disappeared over the top between the rows of jagged broken glass used to prevent intrusion into either property. The bigger lizards with blue-black back, long tail and bright red crest were my favourites to chase.

I climbed the colossal mango tree that stood slightly off-center of the front yard, perched on a substantial branch, surrounded by the elongated leaves; I remembered the stories of snakes being found amongst these very branches. So I was very careful not to go up too far in the tree and looked nervously around. I have always been fascinated yet, frightened by snakes.

These were some of my happiest hours in those days. The familiarity of granny's home unleashed a sensation of abandonment I had lost since I left this place. I jumped to the ground from the last muscular branch and landed on the very spot where my puppy, Sugar would die less than a year later. A large Citroen car which had automatic suspension adjustment would trap Sugar as he took a nap under its shade.

2

I looked back at them, as, from behind the flimsy fencing, they stood waving to me. I waved back. I could see my sister, brother and cousin; their view of my departure obscured by bits of debris that took flight in the light breeze and became stuck on the fence.

And there was my granny's over-generous frame, her stern, caring face re-assuring me. After-all, this was to be my first time ever, on an aero-plane. I walked in line across the tarmac with the other passengers.

Strangely enough, I don't recall being escorted by any British Airways ground staff as we approached. I was 9 years old. Perhaps in those days, it was not considered necessary to ensure that junior passengers boarded the right plane.

The baking sun bullied us as our plane loomed ever larger. I looked around at other planes parked, waiting to carry people off and wing them towards their distant dreams for faraway lands. Some may never reach there, but I did not know of such possible hidden treachery harboured by lady Fate. I had the luxury of innocence and youth.

I had never seen planes close-up before, the nearest had been several hundred feet above me as they buzzed away on their repetitious errands.

We arrived at the foot of the stairs leading up to the ginormous metallic tube shaped like the disgusting cigars my uncle puffed from the extreme corner of his lips. I thought about his wife, my uncaring aunt and her sons and daughters and the house-maid and the life of semi-slavery I had ran away from.

I looked back at the fence and felt courage as I could still make out the forms of my real and more caring family now silently willing me on towards my own adventure, England bound.

I was guided to my seat by a smiling BA cabin crew member. At least they did make sure juniors were led to the correct seat I thought! My fellow passenger occupying the seat next to mine had a kindly face and was probably in her early 20s. My assigned seat was an aisle seat but when she saw me approach with the still smiling attendant, she stood up and let me through, to have her window seat instead.

She probably regretted this kindness later as I must have visited the toilet to pee every half-hour. I had energy and was fuelled by over-excitement at the prospect my new life in a far-off land I had only heard of and that was only because my parents were there.

They had sent for me keeping their unheard promise to send for us once they started to settle in England. I was chosen to be the first to re-join them. Perhaps my luck was finally changing.

The plane progressed bumpily, its giant jet engines throbbed incessantly as they powered the fat aluminum bird over and through wispy clouds as if in a game of hide and seek, in slow motion.

***

After what seemed like forever and a day, I sensed the excitement of other travelers as those that could, were peering through the inadequate windows at the ground ever so far below. I rubbed my eyes with a fist and joined the visual excitement; my pretty and kind seat neighbour was also looking across me out of our window.

The orderly crisscrossing of England's green and pleasant land was now clearly visible from our plane. We dipped lower and lower in stages, almost mimicking the flight of a bird. With each dip, the runway beckoned ever more irresistibly until finally, the plane gave in and bumped grumblingly to the ground and with brakes screeching and the wind roaring past us, we touched ground.

"…welcome to England…and we would like to thank you for …" The flight steward's voice was deep and settling.

***

This time, I was met and led away by a rather portly BA ground staff after I had bid farewell to my seat neighbour and after receiving a pat on the head from the now grinning flight attendant.

After a rather long immigration process where I spent most of the time sat waiting while the immigration agent helped me to process my entry papers, I finally emerged into the passengers meeting hall.

Dazzled by the lights, shy and somewhat bemused, I returned the hugs of my mother first, then my father.

It was at that point that I noticed my father was carrying a baby whom my parents introduced to me as my brother! Whilst in Nigeria, I had not been aware of any siblings abroad.

I was happy, very happy to see my parents and still not sure how I felt about meeting another brother, a very little brother.

My parents looked a lovely couple, mum pretty, dad handsome both dressed smartly and even my newly discovered brother Deji was smartly turned out.

Mum hugged me for so long, perhaps she was trying to drain and absorb the effects of the ill-treatment she heard I had received in the hands of her half-sister and her family.

3

It was Sunday and time for me to return to Chelmsford where I was doing my apprenticeship and part-time study. I usually came home to London every other weekend, when I could afford it. I was 19 and had won a technical apprenticeship position with Marconi Communications Systems, with my father and mother's encouragement. I left school and went to live away from home for the first time. I was fairly self-supporting from that point but of course, mum and dad were always there for when my bank account nudged red.

Marconi owned Chelmsford. It was said that when the workers went home; the town of Chelmsford shut down.

The bus ride to Liverpool Street railway station was uneventful and as per normal. The buzz and busyness surrounded me as I entered the station, starkly contrasting the dull bus trip.

I stopped at a kiosk to get snacks for the fifty minutes train journey. On the way to my train's platform, two Far-East Asian girls standing to one side of the platform gate drew my attention.

They were perhaps 2-3 years older than me, at a guess. The slim, prettier one crossed eyes with me momentarily as I walked past, close by.

I boarded the train and walked along its side corridors, looking for an empty cabin. The train did not seem so full in fact and I was spoilt for choice. I selected one in the carriage before the canteen carriage. I made sure I would be in a carriage which did not get left behind when the train shed some carriages several stations prior to arriving at Chelmsford.

I entered, closed the sliding door dumped my sports bag and guitar on the seat opposite and settled myself into my 'private' cabin.

It was a beautiful spring day and I was relaxed and content with life, not a care in the world and looking forward to the journey back.

I usually preferred to take the train leaving just after 1:30 in the afternoon as it gave me time to settle back into semi-rural life in Chelmsford. I was happy to be returning yet I also looked forward to going home to London whenever the time came.

I had many friends back at the dormitory in Chelmsford, the first 'animal house' I lived in. In fact the whole mansion had been rented by Marconi to house its apprentices and other staff. We always have a lot of fun mixed with rivalry of course. It was a new home offering new experiences and friendships along with challenges academically and socially.

Back home in London, I had my friends from school days whom I saw often when I did go home for weekends. We would play tennis, one of my favourite sports, watch a film, or just lark around town.

There were of course, my two brothers and sister. Two years after I arrived in England, my brother Tunji and sister Demi were also sent for by our parents and journeyed together to England. Demi was 8 years old, even younger than I when I first traveled on a plane. There was approximately 2 years difference between our ages so we were pretty close. Shortly after Tunji and Demi joined me and Deji, our cousin Dotun, who grew up with us at granny's house also left Nigeria, to be with his mother who lived in Scotland at the time.

Normal, sibling rivalry aside, we got on very well and spent a lot of time together and with our friends.

The noise of people walking past the cabin door and along the corridor outside stemmed my daydreaming. Dragging bulky luggage, they bumped into the door which rattled back in protest. I watched them march past my private haven, hoping I will be left alone to continue my reflection during the trip.

I glanced at my watch, wondering if the train was going to leave late as it tends to. Less than five minutes to the scheduled departure time. I stared out of the window across the platforms watching other trains come and go and tried to track the mesmerizing flow of legs striding on the platforms.

I turned as the slide door was disturbed again, this time it was opened. I instantly recognized the pretty girl at the platform gate. She stood behind her slightly plump companion who was not carrying luggage.

"Would you mind if my cousin sits with you, she's still new to the country? She's on her way to White Notley, are you going that far?" The plump girl spoke in a typical but educated London accent. The other girl smiled as her cousin, gave her a reproachful side glance laced with embarrassment.

"Yes, yes of course", I replied, stunned at lady Luck's gift to me. "I'm getting off at Chelmsford, three stops before White Notley"

"Fantastic!" she beamed. "Alright then, call me when you get there won't you?" she said, turning to her delicious cousin and stepping aside to let her into the cabin. I hurriedly pulled my luggage to the seat next to me, making room for her to sit opposite me. She kissed her cousin on the cheek and they hugged. Her cousin smiled an appreciative smile and I returned the smile, even more appreciatively. "Thank you, thank you!" I telepathized with her.

I watched her arrange her luggage and sit down in the opposite seat. Somehow, I sensed this train journey was taking both of us to a destination neither had planned.

We smiled at each other as the train obeyed the departure whistle and chugged effortlessly away from the platform and out of the station.

"I'm Tobi Vaughan and may I ask your name?" I looked at her, she had a cute nose and a great, easy smile with even, white teeth proudly displayed. There was mischief to her eyes too and smooth lightly tanned complexion all wrapped in a slim frame of about 5'6" was so alluring that I almost did not hear her reply.

"Hello, my name is Carlene, Carlene Wang". Close up like this, I thought we might be the same age or she may be a year to two years older max.

I wanted to know everything about this girl and I would be an open book for her, what ever she wanted to know about me, I would oblige.

We talked, I asked her about her cousin and what she had been doing in London and we quickly drifted into easy conversation.

My first and only puppy love had been at primary school when I was around 10 to 11 years old. Her name was Kay Philips. I still think about her to this day but it was puppy love. What I was starting to feel for the girl sitting in front of me was something much more mature and unexpected, certainly not from the dull way my day started on the bus to the train station.

"...I came to spend my weekend with my uncle and aunty in London. They had insisted I come to celebrate my birthday with them!" she said.

"Oh, nice and how was it?" I prompted "Happy belated birthday!"

"Thank you", she gave me that easy smile that I liked so much.

"I had a wonderful time, they are really lovely and it was good to be with family again"

She spoke with a pleasant, lilting accent that seemed all at once familiar yet distant.

"I can't quite place your accent, but it is Far-East Asian isn't it?" I asked.

"Yes, you've got it"; "I'm actually from Kuantan, on the east coast of Malaysia"

"Alright!", "Well I knew it wasn't quite Japanese, that's for sure!" I laughed.

"Come to think of it, you look Chinese, yet you could also pass for a Korean or Japanese too, from certain angles that is!"

"Good thing you didn't say am Japanese, we don't like them much you know", not easy for the Chinese race to forget what they did to us in the past"

I nodded sympathetically.

It was then I remembered. I had heard the same accent once in a movie called Tanamera. One of my favourite stories based in 2nd World-War Singapore and Malaysia. It was inspired by a book of the same title written by Noel Barber.

"So, do you consider yourself Chinese or Malaysian" I asked, genuinely seeking clarification.

"I am a Malaysian Chinese of course". A logical answer to an unnecessary question maybe. "I'm what you might refer to as a third generation Malaysian Chinese" she said this with an emphasized lilt to the words. She beamed her cute smile.

We chuckled and both looked out of the window at the scenery unfolding sideways from urban to suburban to rural. The spring tree blossoms were out in force as if it was their first time ever and birds darted through the trees and over shrubs busily disputing nesting spots or collecting nesting material. Some still had to fight for the right to a mate. There I was hoping mine had been just simply handed to me as I had sat quietly in a train cabin, anticipating another standard journey.

It seemed perfect. It was perfect.

"Please God, let her not have a boyfriend or other distraction" I prayed silently.

Our train slowed as it approached the next stop and the Shenfield station sign sneaked up on us, gliding past the window as we screeched to a halt at the station. We were now a little over half-way towards my stop and I was still grappling with how to get Carlene's number or some contact information of any sort. We had conversed easily after the first awkward moments and yet, the simple question lodged itself in the throat of my mind and just would not come out.

"If you don't mind, can I ask how old you are?" She enquired.

I panicked a little, if I gave the right answer, it might put her off as I would probably be younger than her.

"Happy to tell you if you let me know which birthday you just celebrated!" I quipped, helped out by a shot of bravado.

"You want to play mind games then TV!" She used my nickname with such familiarity I felt bravery re-entering my veins.

"Actually, I'll be 20 this year", It sounded better than telling her am 19 years old!

"I just turned 21 a few days back", she told me and went on to say that her birthday was on 19th April. I immediately filed that safely in my memory. She showed no concern over the fact that I was a little short of 2 years younger than her. Relief crept over me. I was besotted with this girl and didn't want to risk losing her. I wondered if she felt for me even close to what I was starting to feel about her.

I don't know why I had not seen it earlier but she had these rather pretty dimples on her cheeks when she smiled. She had long, stubbornly straight brown-reddish hair all the way down to her hips. Her sweet cotton summer dress paired with a Swiss style waist-coat was set off by stylish ankle boots. The effect was extremely pleasing.

I queried her on life in Malaysia and why she had chosen Black Notley Hospital, of all the hospitals in the world, to come and do her State Registered Nurse or SRN training! I could probably count the population of the villages of Black Notley and White Notley combined on my fingers with a little help from my toes.

But of course, just below the surface, I was happy she had done so. We had already dropped off and collected passengers at Ingatestone station and were now speeding to the next stop, my stop, Chelmsford and I still hadn't plucked up courage to ask what I needed to ask.

"And how about you, what do you do in Chelmsford?"; "My guess is you're a student there. Am I close?" she continued.

"Well yes and more"; I teased. "Actually I study and I work. I'm a trainee for communications engineering on a 'block-release' basis which means the company pays me an allowance, provides accommodation and pays for my course"

"That is a nice deal!"; "In fact it sounds a lot like my SRN program but all our tuition gets done within the hospital. It sounds like yours is in a separate institution"

"Haha, 'institution' makes it sound like my parents sent me to Chelmsford and told them to lock me up and throw the key away!"

We both grinned then laughed out aloud at the thought.

The passing view through the train windows slowly began to crystallize as the blurring of the scenery reduced. I was quickly reminded of my mission impossible.

I didn't even want to leave her and then I had it!

"Carlene, I'd like to see you at least as far as your station, ok?"

"Really?" she asked, needlessly because little did she know I would see her off to the proverbial moon if that was her stop. "Great, but I don't want to inconvenience you!"

“Not a problem at all. Believe me” I assured. I had bought myself more time to get the vital contact number that I craved!

“I was born and raised in Kuantan, in fact even my parents were also born and raised there” She said, continuing from my earlier question about her life in her home country.

“We moved to KL later but I always like going back to Kuantan with my parents on the special occasions. It’s a peaceful coastal town and most of my family and friends are all there of course”

“KL, what does that mean?” I asked.

“Oh, Kuala Lumpur, It’s the capital of Malaysia. Both my parents are academicians. Mum teaches mathematics and Dad was a science professor.”

That would explain the well-raised and educated air she had about her, I thought.

“You said ‘was’ “, I enquired with interest. “Yes, about your dad”

“Oh, dad is not able to work anymore. He hasn’t worked for quite a few years now. Mum struggled hard to raise my two brothers and myself. She still does. After I graduated from secretarial college last year I decided to work abroad and help her financially. My dad’s brother in London helped me to get a trainee position at the hospital.”

I listened intently to her story and sensed sadness interlaced with excitement. Due perhaps to the loss of her father’s lively-hood and the new life she was anticipating in a new country.

“Are you able to tell me what happened?”

“They were in a car accident. Dad suffered paralysis from the waist downwards. Mom had been driving. She’s never driven since although she was not at fault.”

“What happened?”

“They had been hit by an oncoming lorry. The driver had lost control because of failed brakes.”

She paused reflectively.

“Mom blames herself for dad’s injury and is inconsolable to this day, almost 5 years later” She continued.

I wanted to reach out and hug her, tell her it will be ok. I was also conscious that the extra 20 minutes I would gain between my stop and hers had whittled to a mere 2-3 minutes as we neared White Notley station.

"I would love to show you around Chelmsford or maybe we can play tennis sometime?" I blurted out, awkwardly and out of synchronization with the topic. I could only hope the desperation in my voice was evident only to me. 'What a fool, I am'; I thought, wondering if she considered me insensitive, having just shared an inner concern with me and all I could utter was an offer of a date!

"Ok, why not! But I warn you, am not a good player at all" She saved my embarrassment. "I can barely get the ball over the net, anyway, if you get bored with my game maybe you can show me the sights of Chelmsford" She was charming to the point of angelic.

"I can't wait for the game, at last a chance to beat someone at tennis!" I said, modestly. The labouring of the steel wheels finally slowed to a dead stop as 'White Notley!' was announced over the train's public addressing system.

I helped her with her luggage on to the platform and waved to her as she walked towards the station exit. She was about to disappear down the stairs off the platform when she turned around and walked briskly towards me with a grin.

"Hey, how can we contact each other to meet next Saturday?" In my haste I'd forgotten to get her number and she must have wondered how serious I was when I didn't even ask.

I realized I could not remember the Animal House phone number.

"Can I call you?" I asked, finally getting the question out of my head and out there, where it belonged. She gave me her number. "See you at eleven Saturday morning then!" I said happily.

I had even forgotten I had to change to the platform on the other side of the tracks. I walked with her to the exit then turned to get the return train to Chelmsford which rolled up shortly after.

4

Now, years later, sitting in the office, remembering her, I realised more than ever that I have to get back in contact with her. It's not as if I hadn't tried to. It had been an amazing romance but one that had failed a major test ten months into it, "Hey, TV, you're still alright for tennis tonight aren't you?! Barry popped his Winnie the Pooh look-alike head around my office door with a grin on his face, swinging an imaginary racket as he asked. His ginger hair which earned him the nickname 'Carrot-Top' always seemed to have a shaggy look to it. We had been working together for almost three years now and had rapidly become the best of friends. The two of us outwardly, could not have looked more different. Apart from his carrot-coloured locks, he had a freckled pale skinned face which always seemed to have a boyish grin permanently etched on it. He was tall, much taller than Winnie the Pooh but shared the same round face including the tiny eyes and a rotund body. Few people that meet Barry and chat with him failed to like him.

"Bet on it mate, no escape for you this night, last time you won was a pure fluke!"

He'd beaten me narrowly at the last match we played, I was burning for revenge. Being best mates didn't dull our competitiveness. Whenever we played it was guts and blood all the way. He was about to say something but got called away by the secretary.

I was left with my thoughts of Carlene once more and with the weekend starting, I promised myself I'd make an even stronger effort to locate her. Perhaps it was time to try the Internet, it suddenly made perfect sense and I can't think why I never considered it before!

My relationship with Rosemary's been going well, for almost two years now in fact. We met at her house party in South London. She was celebrating her twenty-fifth birthday and the fact that she had just launched her own fashion magazine. Barry had invited me to the party along with a good friend of his that knew Rosemary. I actually had not realized who the party host was on arrival at the house. The celebration; the dancing was well on the way by the time we arrived and the lights were dimmed. The mix of swaying, entwined bodies of couples and strangers was distracting until I caught a glance of a tall slim Indo-Caribbean looking beauty gliding freely amongst the dancers. I watched her head towards the kitchen. Barry and Ronnie, his mate had already drifted into the darkness to mingle. I left the part of the wall which I had been propping up and headed for the kitchen, certain in my purpose; unclear as to how to achieve it.

She was busy setting out more finger food and drinks on the large oval table aided by three other girls. She looked in charge and she looked at home. I later found out she *was* at home and that she was the celebrant.

***

We had our first date the following weekend. She had been busy with the magazine but managed to squeeze out some time for us to have coffee in the West End area of Central London. Her magazine's publisher where she had just attended a meeting was only around the corner in Bloomsbury Square.

"Are you always this gorgeous looking Rosemary?" I had asked her as she arrived and I stood up to let her sit down first.

"Thanks but how's a girl supposed to answer that without sounding vain or coy Tobi?" she asked in her ever so pleasant sing-song Caribbean accent, flashing me a wide grin that released a flash of evenly arranged pearl-white teeth. Through the floor to ceiling glass window of the coffee shop, I had watched her approach. Although she was only wearing a pair of light blue jeans and a white blouse with flared cuffs, she drew or should I say, she 'drooled' attention from passing guys who had to do a double take to believe what their eyes was feasting on. Her long black hair and fine features reminded me of Iman, a super model from Ethiopia who married David Bowie. In Rosemary's case, her paralyzing looks were a gift from her mixed parentage of a black West Indian father and a Sri Lankan West Indian mother. Her smooth dark brown skin willed one to touch and caress it; risking a slap and handbag in the face no doubt.

But she's not Carlene, not fair on her I suppose but ever since Carlene, no one's been good enough somehow.

The phone rang, "Mr. Vaughan, there's a call from the travel agency…?", "yes, thank you" I answered the unspoken question. I'd almost forgotten my business trip was due in less than a week from now. My first ever visit to an Asian country. After the call, I spun the seat 90 degrees and gazed at the busy square below, London Docks is a great location to work in but my heart was drifting again and my mind followed, faithfully as I stared without seeing.

Previous attempts to contact her had been in vain in one way or other.

The closest I came was a hint from Heather, Carlene's cousin from the first meeting. Luckily I had kept the number because Carlene always stayed with them whenever she was in London. That is, except the one time she stayed with my family and me for a weekend.

***

It was awesome. I took her on her first real tour around London, as I knew it. We went during my favourite season too. The golden colours and the warm, cozy glow of the sun was abound as the rays ricocheted off the autumn leaves. We spent hours in Hyde Park. She wore a knee-length black dress with lime green leaf motif and black leather boots that rose to her knees and a smile so bright and her long black hair was pony-tailed and hung down close to her waistline. She'd returned to her natural hair colour.

I had on, a pair of brown bear colour corduroy trousers and a loose fawn cotton shirt; we looked great together and moreover, we felt great together and I really did feel the luckiest guy ever. We walked and talked, played with the nervously inquisitive squirrels. We took photos posing between trees of oak, chestnuts and my all-time favourite tree, the weeping willows that were over-hanging a pond in the park.

As the evening fell, before we knew it, we were at Piccadilly Circus by the Hippodrome and the bright lights of the square were already coming to life.

Although Eros was no longer peeing in the fountain, his statue and the fountain in which it stood were still as popular as ever with tourists and Londoners alike.

I asked a young German couple to take pictures of us with the little 'pee-master' while being careful to avoid his aim in case he regains energy to play 'water-pistols' again!

Carlene then returned the photo-taking favour for the touring couple.

The cinemas and theatres were doing a bustling trade as people queued up to see the latest preview shows and premiers. There was always the chance to glimpse celebrities who turned up for the premiers. This 1-mile square, centered on Leicester Square, has until this day remained one my favourite night spots in London. It was 24-hours on the go and at night the energy only increases driven by a mix of Londoners and tourists all seeking the same thing, fun and something memorable to tell the folks back home! Artistic street entertainers of various degrees of skills added to the allure.

Holding hands, we slipped between the crowds along the narrow streets of Soho and headed for China Town. I wasn't much of a connoisseur when it came to Chinese cuisine but I figured I'd let Carlene decide (I just hoped I could afford whatever place she chose for us to eat at).

After what seemed like an endless series of windows displaying crucified, crispy ducks all hung by the neck, we found a place we both liked. The food and ambience was exquisite; perhaps it makes a difference when your girlfriend can converse in Cantonese dialect with the chef!

'Girlfriend', it had a very nice ring to it. I'd come what seemed a long way since the first day of meeting and my choked attempt at getting her number! Now we walked, talked and teased like we grew up together. That was how smooth our relationship had rapidly become.

Something moved and caught my eye; I jumped as my mobile phone buzzed across the polished surface of the desk, making a weird, droning sound. "Come on, chop-chop then", Barry's voice sabotaged my thoughts. "Meet you down at the car park in what, 5 minutes?"

***

Sitting in front of the television that night; I fiddled with the remote control. I was beaming with pleasure at the revenge I wreaked on my luckless best friend Barry. Driven by some inner frustration, he stood no chance and I walked from the courts barely stopping myself from doing my Alice in Wonderland click-your-heels-in-the-air impression. Just to rub it in for Barry!

But, something else was making me fiddle. I abandoned the Janet Jackson music video and headed for the other virtual world, the Internet.

I decided to try my luck at finding her on the Internet. It is the largest library in the world after all.

In less than 30 minutes, defeated by the humongous data overload from over zealous search engines and with eyes radiating tears from the onslaught, I sought refuge in a Malaysian online chat room. After all, she had said Kuantan was a small town and better to start at the root right?

5

Heather had suggested Carlene maybe be back in Malaysia but could not be certain, I had a feeling she was protecting her cousin somehow.

I thought of how we broke up and tried to put my finger on exactly when the break-up actually started. Was it when she called me and in an unusually tensed tone, asked me if it was ok for her to attend an army's party? It was organized by the US Army based some miles away from her hospital where she trained. Or perhaps it was some weeks earlier, when she was in my arms as we laid on the soft summer grass in the park in Chelmsford, oblivious to the playful crowd who were also enjoying the bright weather in the open air. As we talked on that summer's day, she had dropped a strong hint that she wanted us to get married or at least a commitment to each other by engagement. As a 19 year old, talking with a girl 2 years older about engagement and marriage, I blew it with my incoherent answers.

I just wasn't ready and that much was clear to her. She masked her disappointment and I didn't think that much of it anymore.

But I was to pay the price by losing the coolest girl I never knew I had.

When she asked if I was ok with her going to the party, she told me there had been a general invitation sent by the army guys to the nurses at the hospital. I was naive for sure but I was also poked by a mixed sense of guilt and not wanting to show her I was a jealous kind of guy. That I didn't feel insecure with her as my heart held on by a string.

"Yes of course it's ok", I said, smiling down the phone to her.

"Sweetheart, are you sure?" She asked.

"Yep, could I get an invitation too?" I joked. "I love you TV and I promise to be good!" She replied and I could almost feel her glow through the phone.

***

To this day I still remember the sense of dread that followed the call. And with good reason too.

Less than 2 weeks later she told me about 'Bob' whom she'd met at the party and although I played it cool but inside I was a volcanic blend of jealousy, sense of loss, insecurity and inadequacy.

After all, 'Bob' was in a real job and as an American was a better 'catch' as she had told me how her mum had always instilled a feeling that Western guys, especially Americans were the best of the bunch for a girl to marry.

Not only this but 'Bob' had a car albeit a Peugeot 206 but at least he had a car unlike me who was riding a Yamaha 250cc around. I'd only recently got the bike too after buying it broken and unloved from my old-school mate Peter Pocock, Pee Pee for short at school. And yes, we pulled his legs silly about it! I'd fixed the lifeless bike after dragging it one night from his home and on the train and from the train station in Chelmsford all the way back to the Animal House. I worked tirelessly on it until it burst into life again after some days. I even got it past the M.O.T. road-worthiness test and insured it. My pride and joy!

Until I found out about 'Bob' that is.

That week we broke up. I gathered all the beautiful letters she wrote me, the cards, the photos and I took them back to her. Thinking I would somehow get semblances of revenge for her deciding to date Bob and not me any longer. I could see the deep hurt in her eyes the day I sat in her room at the nurses' residence.

I gave back all memories that were the reason I was so happy and so proud to have her as my girlfriend, much to the envy of the Animal House inmates. And later, my house mates after I moved out of the Animal House.

I had no feeling of happiness on returning all these things, rather, my action was a double-edged sword, and I had only managed to pierce both our hearts. She cried soft tears, mine welled up behind my eyes but I hung on. She hadn't actually wanted to break up with me but rather, wanted to be friends with Bob. I felt I could see where it would lead so I let go, before I was let go. Perhaps I made what I dreaded, come to pass. Either way, it was the loneliest walk I ever made as I left her room. I never remembered the ride back home which was a good 30 minutes at least. But I remembered the beautiful grounds of the hospital were cloaked in autumn leaves and irony finally pushed out the tears as I walked reluctantly to the bike. I didn't dare to look back as I knew I would see her at the window. That's how Carlene was, loving till the end.

The same sensation of regret that I had the next day still haunts me to this moment.

How could I have made such a mistake? Why didn't I fight for her? Perhaps I did, in the way I knew then. Within two weeks of our break-up, I had part-exchanged my bike for a car, a silver Ford Mondeo with a sun-roof.

I had been given a good deal with my bike and after a little work on the car, had it road-ready including insurance but I hadn't received a full driving license. I had taken a few driving lessons with Rangit an Indian friend at work. He was licensed but didn't have a car and happened to live in London, on the way to my home. He would sit with me during our trips back to London so we were legal until I dropped him off and was then on my own all the way home.

I bought the car because I felt it would help me win Carlene back. Typical male chauvinistic line of thinking but that's what I concluded. One day after gathering courage and locking up my pride, I drove to her home. We hadn't talked on the phone since that day of the break-up except for a call she made to say she had written my mother a letter explaining that we had parted, the way she said it made me feel two things. First, she really did like and felt close to my mother. Second, I sensed she had done this to get my attention because she too did not want to let go completely.

Yet, I wanted her back and to be all mine without any 'Bob' in the picture at all. Arriving at the nurses' residence, I could hear the sumptuous crunch of the bed of crispy autumn leaves as my car wheels rolled over them.

I was careful to park the car right where she would see it from her bedroom window.

I hoped she would be in. As I remembered her duty roster meant she should be. Yet, who knows, maybe she would be out with 'him'.

I took the chance and I struck lucky, she opened the door at my second tentative knock. We both gave each other an awkward smile and were caught in an uncomfortable yet, familiar situation that only two once-upon-a-time lovers could empathise with.

We talked but I can hardly remember what about. I longed to just have things as they were, warm, easy-going, deeply loving and carefree. Now it was all gone and the air was tense when in the same place at a different time, we had expressed love and passion neither of us had known, yet we never made love.

The thought of him taking my princess whom I had respected and never pushed into having sex with really hurt. It was too much to bear. He was her first man, yet I was her first real love. I remember breaking from these thoughts and telling her about my new toy parked downstairs. I remember guiding her to the window and telling her the story of how I bought it and my risky trips to and from between London and Chelmsford.

"It's lovely Tobi, really very nice", she said it as if she meant it. However, she declined my invitation to go for a ride in it with me.

I knew it wasn't because I had no license, rather the reason ran deeper.

Shortly after that visit, she told me they were engaged and would be going to America to get married and to live.

My heart cried, long before I could. I cared for nothing, lost any focus I had on work or college. My interest in the car fizzled away. Endless days of existing but not living followed and turned into weeks. I wrote songs about her and played them on my guitar and only deep-seated pride prevented me from going to see her again, unannounced. Then the calls stopped although mine continued but unanswered. Finally, one of her friends put me out of my misery temporarily after she informed me that Carlene had gone to the US after graduating and will marry there.

My emotions were that of a gladiator on his knees, once loved by the emperor and the crowd but now about to receive the 'thumbs down' at the hands of defeat by a new and gallant crowd champion.

***

I wanted her more than ever. Ironically, this thought reminded me of my promise to Rosemary to go dancing tonight.

I really wasn't in the mood and I called her and made an excuse but I knew she would be ok because she would join the girls' night out with her friends anyway. Cupid had me where it hurts and he wasn't doing it for Rosemary who is really a lovely woman. I always did feel guilty that I harbour a secret love of the past. She knew of it but never felt threatened because she knew Carlene was out of my reach and she knew I genuinely cared very much about her. If I had sensed any sadness from her because I couldn't meet her tonight, I would have made myself go and the night would have probably turned out ok. We have good times together usually and never seem to quarrel.

Replacing the phone on its stand, I looked back at the screen and saw a message box flashing:

Sarah_HK says: Hi, r u there la?

I hesitated, still caught up in the reminiscence. Then I decided to respond.

West_End_Guy says: Hey, what's up? Where're you from?

Sarah_HK says: Hong Kong and u?

Sarah_HK says: can u send me your photo?

West_End_Guy: yeah ok but can we exchange?

I waited for her reply and watched the endless flow of nonsensical banter going on in the chat channel; occasionally I would see my nick name in the stream of text as someone unknown to me would address me. The topic of discussion listed by the chat room owner or controller was left completely unheeded as the battle of words ensued. The chaos was joined every now and then by wondering virtual beings that floated into the room and left once disinterest hit them. Some would take part some would observe like vultures looking to get their next meal of virtual sexual gratification or just simply looking for company to help pass an otherwise bland and tasteless evening, morning, noon or night.

Sarah_HK say: I have cam what about u?

West_End_Guy says: Nope, I don't have, sorry. Want my photo now? Can I see your webcam?

Sarah_HK says: yup, send it to me, wait, let's go to Yahoo, do you have it? My ID is the same and what's urs?

West_End_Guy says: ok I'll add you, hold on….

I logged into Yahoo messenger and clicked to add her ID on my miserable looking buddy list of 8 contacts 3 of whom were family the other five included Rosemary and Barry and we hardly ever chatted since we met often.

Although I couldn't see her online, I received her message shortly.

Sarah_HK says: hi, that's better right?!

West_End_Guy says: yeah it sure is! Ok so now you have me here, what would you like to do with me?

I flirted with her sensing she was in a very good mood.

Sarah_HK says: Oh, hey I see ur photo now in your profile, very nice la. I like black guys, I had a friend who was black, and he used to work here in Hong Kong.

I wondered if her friend is still black since he 'was black'. Who knows, right?

She continued:

Sarah_HK says: where did you say you are now?

West_End_Guy says: in London, UK. I'll send my photo now. I took this one about a year ago.

I waited for her to receive the file I was sending.

West_End_Guy says: got it yet?

Sarah_HK says: ye thanks u looks high!! I'm so short, more than you and you looks so cool with the glasses.

West_End_Guy says: haha thanks, am not that tall, just about 6'2" what about you?

Sarah_HK says: my god too high la! No way, secret, won't tell you hehehe.

We chatted for maybe another quarter of an hour, mostly

personal questions about each other then I remembered an earlier question still unanswered:

West_End_Guy says: hey Sarah so can I see you now, on your cam?

Sarah_HK says: you know something Tobi, you're hot, I think black guys are hot man! Can you see me?

West_End_Guy says: not yet, I just got your invitation.

I accepted her invitation to view her cam and waited for eternity until her cam image came up and wow what an image!

She was a cute looking Chinese girl maybe in her mid to early 20s; she had said she's 24 years old. Her glossy black hair hung down her back on one side and her front on the other, just covering one of her otherwise naked breasts. Her large, dark brown, pert nipple peeked generously from within its veil of black hair strands. Her other breast was in clear view, she was naked, at least wearing no bra, no blouse no nothing upstairs! She was relaxed and sensual. She did not say or type a word further. She simply took her time caressing herself from the shoulders down, occasionally swept her fingers through her hair then back to her body, down her abdomen towards goodness knows where. Then I knew where. She stood up and brushed her pubic hairs so close to the cam I was surprised it didn't steam the lenses up. My eye lids were popping and yeah down below, the not-so-little monkey was growing up fast and paying serious attention too.

I saw her hand reach out and the cam moved as she sat down and pointed it and gave me a clear view of what I envisaged the first man must have confused with the gates to heaven! And the gates were glistening with fresh evening dew one might say.

Yet all too soon, she was gone. Suddenly, the cam closed. No image, no message and no more Sarah. I frantically sent messages to her but never received a reply. She was really gone.

The monkey was pissed.

I stared at the screen and replayed the images in my mind. If I ever thought it couldn't have happened, the tensed and hardworking muscles in my loins told a different and very real story. It did happen and I did react and was turned on by a first-time-experience of virtual whatever-it-is-you-want-to-call-it!

Subconsciously, I vowed to keep trying to contact her, which then reminded me very consciously that I was looking for Carlene. Bang to reality.

I searched in Yahoo and MSN using her full name, her last name and her first name all in various combinations including with her location, age, gender etc.

I added a few that looked like remote possibilities and waited to see what would happen. There was no guarantee that the IDs were still in use by the owners or that even if they are in use, that any is online at the moment.

I sent a brief message of introduction to three that seemed closest and enquired if they were the Carlene.

Meanwhile, the banal dialogue in the chat room continued unabated. I watched for a while and thought again and again about the cute and sexy Sarah. Unashamedly, I even searched for her using her nickname in MSN but to avail.

I joined the aimless chit-chat and even had some private chats but all were along the same lines, 'what's ur name', 'where're u from?', 'how old are u?', 'asl', 'Are you single or married?' etc. Then, in a world where distraction is the name of the game and where a short span of attention is a pre-requisite for success and pleasure, I found myself first, invited then very quickly, drawn in.

At the flick of a finger I traveled from one time zone, past my own and swung to the other extreme with ease. I chatted with people in the USA, Spain, and Turkey right over to Australia. And all this was done in the space of a few minutes of keyboard bashing. That's just a little less time than it took in Jules Verne's Around the World in Eighty Day's novel.

I received an answer from one of my searches. She said her English name is Gina; she came up in my search because she had the same Chinese name as Carlene, Lingling.

She was born and raised in Malaysia but her parents are originally from mainland China. I found out later that she'd had a traumatic childhood:

LinglingG says: are you really in England at the moment?

She continued after we'd got past the standard self-introductions.

West_End_Guy says: yes of course, what makes you ask? You seem to doubt it.

LinglingG says: well you know a lot of men lie online.

West_End_Guy says: and women don't right?

LinglingG say: how did u find me then?

***

I returned two weeks later from my uneventful business trip to Asia. True, Indonesia and Singapore were an incredible experience and I definitely want to return there sometime in the future. From a business perspective, it was a success yet uneventful because I had somehow hoped for something new personally.

Sitting and relaxing with colleagues on the beach in Bali we had shared stories including some Internet ones. Sujatha, our marketing manager from the Kuala Lumpur office announced her recent engagement. When asked how they both met, her answer was shy but quite matter-of-fact:

"We met on the Internet"

"You mean through a mail-order type of service?" Barry asked tactlessly but without ill-intent.

Then the debate started as to the merits and demerits of Internet dating and moved on to the kind of people we've met online. I shared some of my own online stories but left out the more stimulating details of the encounter with Sarah from Hong Kong.

But I did tell them about LingLingG who had suffered habitual rape by her father from a very early age until she was in her early 20s when she was finally able to leave home and Malaysia to go to mainland China. She of course hates her family especially her mother who was passive through such a traumatic experience at the hands of her own father.

She had mentioned I was one of a very few she had talked to about this and the first online.

I had no reason to doubt her. I saw nothing she would gain by lying about such an experience. In fact she had confided in me a few days later only after a lot of encouragement when I realised something was quite wrong.

I couldn't help but wonder how many such abuse went

unchecked and un-reattributed.

Alone in the hotel room, particularly in Singapore where I had more time it dawned on me that the online route was not for me. It also wasn't going to help me with Carlene I concluded.

Then I knew what I had to do. Write a book!

6

It was a per usual gloriously sunny day in Clearwater, Florida and Carlene's drive to work this morning had been pleasant and relatively uneventful. The warm moisture-laden air caressed her hair as she drove her Peugeot convertible with a clear view of the gorgeous Floridian beach. She thought how she had never regretted leaving the cold state of North Dakota for the warm and sultry southern one of Florida. So much of the climate here reminded her of her hometown in the seaside resort of Kuantan on the eastern coast of Malaysia. The years of struggle she had put into part-time study to qualify as a medical doctor whilst raising a hyper-active daughter, making a home and caring for her husband had also been worth it.

Today was her special day and though it arrives with impeccable regularity each year, she always looked forward to it and makes an effort to make it stand out.

"Hey Dr. Wang; my, my don't you look fine and on top of the world today!"

"Good morning Dr. Lamont, thank you and how're you today? She returned the grin beamed at her by Lamont, a physician colleague with a smooth-talking reputation that ran way ahead of him at Tampa Bay Memorial Hospital. Some would say the female nurses also ran way ahead of him at the slightest hint that he might be around.

"Well you know how much better I get when I see you and even when you turn your back on me and walk away I get a high" Lamont drawled, leeringly.

"Are you getting high again Doctor, you need to stay away from the medicine cabinet!" Carlene teased as she walked away towards her ward. "And don't be looking at my back, I can already feel your eyes burning me up"

"You and me Doc, don't fight the inevitable, it's nature's way. You and me"

She greeted her colleagues in the ward and went to see her favourite patient before starting her rounds.

"I see that Lemon's got yo' back again Dr. Carlene" Mrs. Patterson said with more than an air of indignation. "He outa go find him-self a rotten ol' tree and park his teenie-weenie banana there!" She continued in her comical southern accent that Carlene loved so much.

"Don't he know you already got yo'self a fine white boy?"
Carlene giggled girlishly as she gave Mrs. Patterson a hug and smiled at her use of Lamont's hospital wide-nickname.

"Mrs. Patterson, you are so mischievous, you shouldn't call him by that name"

"Yeah well, Lemon by name, character and size, you know!" the fragile looking elderly lady quipped and grinned through gums that no longer bore the burden of sprouting denture.

"How is yo' Bobby and pretty lil' Megan?" She enquired.

Carlene was about to reply when she noticed the ward had gone silent and the staff that had been all around the ward moments earlier had all disappeared. She called to her ward colleagues but there was no reply from the ward office.

"Just a moment Mrs. Patterson, I'll be right back"

She walked slowly to the closed office door which was usually open wide. As she opened the door a curtain of coloured confetti showered down on her and a loud cheer of "Surprise!"; "Happy Birthday!" from her colleagues that had been hiding in wait. A spontaneous chorus of the 'birthday song' was struck. She was truly surprised and her pleasure and happiness was clear as day for all in the room to see. Even 'Lemon' was there.

They presented her with a combined gift and cards.

She blew out the candles on the cake amid the cheering.

"Go ahead Carlene, open it!" she was encouraged by all in the office. The package was large and heavy but with help, she managed to place it on the desk.

Ripping open the wrapping she revealed a lovely 1 meter high grandfather clock in what appeared to be mahogany wood frame and glistening gold-plated clock face and pendulum.

She thanked them all deeply as they heartily gauged into the fruit-topped birthday cake.

"Happy birthday again lovely lady from the mysterious Far-East, look what I've got for you"

Carlene didn't need to turn around to know who was behind her. Mrs. Patterson had only just finished berating him in his absence. She did turn and Lamont stood there with a small package in his extended hands.

"It's for you; I found it in a bookshop last week"; "It seemed so appropriate" Lamont continued.

"Dr. Lamont, thank you but you really shouldn't have".

"Maybe so but I did!"; "It's ok, open it" he incited.

She knew there was no such thing as a 'free lunch'. Accepting this present from him would only encourage him but she was intrigued and like most women, loves a surprise. It was clearly a book and the paper wrapping was neat with a small tagged card saying 'Happy Birthday Carlene, You Know Who'.

"Hmmm, don't I just" she thought.

She pulled the book away from the torn wrapping. The simple book title sent a thrill and chill through her; 'Carlene'.

The early morning birthday surprise by her husband Bob and 7-year old daughter Megan had been special and the beautiful Cartier watch from Bob and the cute Hello Kitty hand-bag from Megan were wonderful and yet, this gift from her persistent but unwanted admirer had created the strongest, most immediate emotional impact.

***

At home later that night, she pulled out the book gifted her earlier in the day. It was a novel, a romance.

She hadn't dared to tell Bob that Lamont had been responsible for the gift. Bob strongly disliked him. She had thought of returning the gift and getting her own copy but it would have been rather impolite she had decided.

Carlene thought about the surprise by her colleagues and how Mrs. Patterson had played her part so well by keeping her distracted with her outbursts about Lamont.

It has to be said that; Mrs. Patterson certainly knows how to tell it like it is or should be! She thought.

Flipping the book to the back cover, she read the story description. Chills radiated from her neck down her spine. She started to read the story of 'Carlene', her name-sake after whom, the book was entitled.

As the words turned smoothly into imagery and the imagery into emotions, she felt like the author was holding her hand and walking her through a distant past that she had constantly fought to suppress recollection of. For each time the memories surfaced, sentiments of regret followed close behind. It's not at all fair to Bob and certainly not to her gift from God, her daughter Megan.

Although the 'Carlene' in the story is from the Caribbean island of Grenada but there was a parallel of her story to hers, Carlene felt. She had also been a trainee nurse in England, as had the leading female character of the book. Could it be simply 'coincidence?' Maybe but an incredible one!

Driven by uncontrollable curiosity, she had read quite a long way into the novel when she decided to see who the author was. The name, Scipio Moore didn't mean anything to her. She read the profile of the author and the jumble of words, imagery and emotions instigated by the story floated around in her head and settled peacefully into a picture so clear, so real and yet so distant. She could no longer suppress the inevitable.

She knew who the book was based on and who had crafted this novel that she had felt so connected to.

Her first thought was to call the publisher for Tobi's contact details. She was dazed; she still could not believe that after so long, almost 10 years, she could feel so strongly connected to Tobi and that she was still so deep in his heart as to inspire his first novel. It had just been published according to the details in the book.

Carlene was truly stunned but despite her heart imploring her to make the call, she resisted. After all, she has a family now. A happy family she told herself.

Although Bob had been a wonderful provider, loving husband and father for her daughter, they did have some problems.

It had all come to a head 4 months ago on New Year's Eve when their mostly peaceful marriage had been rocked to its very foundations.

Yet, somehow they had managed to get over this anything-but-small bump on their way to marital bliss. As per the very definition of life, it was not all over. There was more to come that would ultimately test the endurance of their matrimony.

7

Normally, she found it would take her quite a while to get into a novel and its subliminal plots. She often even had to force herself to 'stick with it' and resist the temptation to skip ahead. This novel was different. Carlene savoured every sentence as she poured through recognisable recollections of an earlier romantic adventure that started on a train.

In fact, she clearly remembered it had started on a train station platform of a distant city far from where her life had now brought her.

He had something different about him as he walked tall and straight with his guitar swung over his right shoulder and his 2-wheeled weekend/sports bag dragged behind with his left hand. He was dressed casually in a sports track-suit. Carlene had summed him up as an easy-going, sporty, neat yet artistic type. The bag style and the guitar seemed to give that away. He couldn't have been much older than her she thought.

It was incredible to see how fate works at times. Had their future meeting been planned and designed at the very moment when they shared a fleeting glance at each other on that lovely spring day?

Electing to do her training in England as opposed to continuing her career in Malaysia had not been easy.

She had re-assured her parents, her mother whom she was very close to, in particular, she would return after 9-months to visit them. She would then return to England to complete her 2-year nursing training so far away.

Then there was also her ex-boyfriend, Stuart Wong who had been pressing her to come back to her and forgive his indecisiveness flavoured by his womanising tendencies. True, he was a magnet for sophisticated, go-getting, gold-digging girls in KL with his charming boyish looks not to mention the wealth accrued by his affluent parents, typical of the high-society Chinese-Malaysians.

They had been child-hood sweethearts and had attended the same secondary school and everyone that mattered had just expected they would marry ultimately. All that changed when, after 2 years of delaying fulfilling his promise that they would get engaged; he parked his pig style tail between his fat legs and ran off to Brisbane in Australia. Supposedly, he went for further studies despite pleading with him and many nights when her tears literally woke her up.

She had always been sensitive and expressive; characteristics Stuart often said he loved about her but which was to bury her in a cloak of gloom under which she shared space with loneliness as her companion for months after.

Fair to say that he had written to her often, she had of course replied. His letters had been initially re-assuring and soothing. Letting her know he still returns her love and would get her over to Australia as soon as he could.

Then the tone and frequency of the letters changed, less romantic protestations, less letters and finally the revelation.

He was in love and living with a Japanese fellow student who he said heavily depended on him and needed him and he couldn't help himself. Yeah, right! Carlene thought to herself. She also knew he would have a lot of 'fun' persuading his parents to let their only son marry a Japanese girl.

Carlene remembered actually she felt sorry for the girl as she certainly was in for a major wake-up call regarding Chino-Japanese 'no-no's. That is, if her parents would even let her discuss the subject of Stuart in the first place.

She heard Megan's voice calling her from her bedroom up-stairs, and she clawed herself away from the book, placed it face down at the page she was reading and went to attend to her daughter, woken up by a nightmare.

***

She later returned to the novel after making sure that Megan was settled in her sleep again.

Though she was reading the story, her parallel thoughts of the past were somehow triggered by aspects of what she was reading. Her fondest memories rushed back and seemed fresh and clear in spite of her attempts at suppression all these years.

Of course, the story did not depict their romance verbatim but she could track and follow the threads that told their true experience hidden within the plot of the novel.

The amazing times they had spent together in London, the parks, the quiet times, long walks and even tennis games. She had actually even won a few games although she suspected sportsmanship from Tobi for letting her win.

She had of course been shown around London by her cousin yet seeing the old city through the eyes of her once-upon-a-time love was a completely different experience. Almost indescribable tranquility when they walked the parks and then the buzz that typified a cosmopolitan city like London when they reached the Piccadilly and Leicester Square areas.

She even remembered their first real Chinese meal together.

Yes, they had eaten Chinese take-away food in Chelmsford but that hardly compared to the real thing in China Town London.

She laughed out when she thought of the comical Christian heart-crossing Tobi had made as they passed the racks of roasted ducks strung up at restaurant windows there.

He said he wanted to ward off the evil of the chefs that would do such a thing yet he licked his lips at the delicious Mandarin Duck dish they ordered shortly after!

They had definitely been an unusual and attractive couple as they breezed easily through the narrow streets but then, London was full of unusual couples and they felt at home. Somewhat different from the stares of admiration, disapproval and sheer jealousy they had experienced on occasion in rural Chelmsford and Black Notley.

She was in love, they were in love and anyone with eyes that worked could see. She regretted her part in bringing their romance to such an abrupt end. She in fact had blamed herself solely. She had been overly sensitive about indecisiveness given her history with Stuart. When Bob popped the question without hesitation shortly after their meeting she felt she couldn't lose the chance by waiting for Tobi who was still finding his feet.

On reflection, it was a callous and perhaps cold decision to take but she was guided by standards drilled into her by her parents to not let opportunities slip by. She knew it would also have been a tough battle to get parental approval even if Tobi had been ready. In the end Bob was definitely more acceptable to her family.

He was also a nice person basically so she had thought 'why not'. The chance to move to the USA was also attractive to her.

8

All in all, Carlene had been happy and satisfied with the path she had chosen for her life with Bob. That was until she found him in bed with his Hispanic ex-girlfriend, Satana or 'Satan' as Mrs. Patterson refers to her. Apart from Mrs. Patterson, Heather, her cousin was the only other person Carlene had told about her husband's infidelity. She had to tell someone and telling Heather was natural as they were best of friends but Mrs. Patterson had dragged it out of her one day when she was working a nightshift. She was in the ward office and had been on the phone to Bob and the topic of Satana came up again despite the fact that she was one of the reasons Bob had agreed to their move to Florida, away from North Dakota.

Mrs. Patterson had come to look for her for a chat and must have noticed she was unhappy about something. In her irrepressible manner, she coaxed the reason from Carlene. But strangely, she held Satana responsible, not Bob of whom she would not hear a bad word spoken.

Carlene and Bob were still living in North Dakota then and on a bitterly cold New Year's Eve night; they were supposed to attend a party at their friends' house close by. Bob had mentioned he needed to stop by the office for some hours but he would be back in time for them to go to the party. Megan was staying with her grandparents for a few nights. Waiting alone at home for her husband, Carlene started to get concerned at the lateness. She wondered many things including the possibility that Bob had been involved in a road accident or something. She called his cell phone several times and his direct office line as the reception was already closed for the seasonal break.

She couldn't get an answer on either phone.

She called her parents-in-law and tried to sound as casual as she could as she enquired whether Bob had talked to them that day. He hadn't. She waited a little longer and then she couldn't stand it further, her mind a mix of worry and suspicion, she drove towards her parents-in-law's house just 20 minutes drive away. She drove past the house looking for signs of his car parked in the driveway or nearby in case he had stopped by since her call to his parents. There was no sign of his car.

***

Having driven aimlessly for a while, without a clue as to what her next steps should be, she stopped her car by the roadside momentarily, to gather her thoughts. Then it crossed her mind to check the house of his ex-girlfriend who had been bugging him recently to return to her. They had a love child and she still considers him 'hers' despite their break-up several years ago and the fact that he was married.

Cruising slowly over the crunchy snow in her car along the road where Satana lived with her daughter, she could barely make out the shape of her husband's blue Ford Explorer. It was parked almost directly outside the house Satana lived in. The car was shrouded by the fresh snowfall of the day.

Carlene's pulse raced. How long she sat in her parked car, outside the house, she could not remember. Yet she did glance at the dashboard clock showing almost 11:30pm, 30 minutes to go, to a new year full of hopes and fresh dreams. But her husband was very likely to be inside this house, with another woman and she was supposed to have been waiting for him at home to go to a party to see a new year in.

She had been held captive in her own car indeterminately by indecision. There was a hesitation as to whether to go in or go home. This may not be the first time they've been together since their marriage and if so, she didn't know before and everything was ok. Perhaps the best thing is to just turn and go home and pretend she never was here, outside this house.

She had left the engine running to keep the heater on and she decided to pull away and go home. It's still a mystery to her until this day, as to how Carlene found herself knocking at the door of Satana's house.

As she waited, she turned and saw her car's engine was still running from the steam out of the exhaust and the lights were on. It had not moved.

A young woman in her late twenties opened the door.

"Yes, can I help you?" she enquired in a foreign, perhaps European accent.

"Hi, are you Satana?" Carlene had never seen Satana's photo and had not encouraged Bob to discourse her origins or anything about her in actual fact. So she had no idea what she would look like.

"No, I am not, sorry. I am her lodger. Tenant you say. You want to come in? I will fetch her for you" she offered politely.

"No, no, it's ok, thank you. But, tell me, is Bob here?" Carlene's voice quivered and she hoped it was not noticed by the tall and pretty foreigner.

"Ah yes, Bob, he is here too yes. Ok come in, too cold outside."

She gestured an inviting hand to Carlene who stepped uncertainly into the house.

"You can knock on the door of the first room on the right upstairs, they are inside. Oh; Happy New Year to you!" she was sweet.

"Thank you so much, I wish you the same, Happy New Year to you too" The lack of lustre and warmth to Carlene's replied greeting must have passed un-noticed as the girl smiled widely and turned to continue watching the TV show.

With trepidation she climbed the never-ending steps that could not have been more than fifteen.

The door was slightly open but she decided to knock even though it was almost as if she could see through the door. The knock was more to give herself time, than the naked couple that lay in Satana's bed that night. She knew what to expect as she opened the door when Satana's voice invited. She saw what she expected as she stood at the open doorway staring at her husband and his ex-girlfriend in their nakedness barely covered by a hurriedly grasped satin bed sheet that wrapped them both.

The inner strength she found to help herself get over such a telling night is beyond her comprehension. She had dug deep into her reserves of patience and forgiveness but she let her body weep not just her eyes. And not just her heart as her body convulsed in sorrow. Memories of Stuart and his single line letter informing her of his Japanese girlfriend made the pain deeper. It was not the first time she had been let down by someone she loved and totally relied on.

Now, two years on, they were ploughing a new life away from the bad memories.

But the book that lay on her lap was asking questions she hadn't wanted to face since leaving England.

What if I had stayed with Tobi? And what if Megan was mine and Tobi's and we lived in England instead? She shocked herself that after so many years of marriage, she was having such retrospection. She had no answer and she didn't want to spoil the new chance she and Bob had created for themselves.

Then it dawned on her that perhaps a major reason she was able to forgive her husband for his adultery was that she could understand his situation with his ex-girlfriend. She couldn't help wondering how she would be if Tobi lived in the same city as she and Bob.

As in the case of her husband and Satana, according to his long and pleading explanation later, it hadn't been a clean ending to the break-up for her and Tobi. The fabric of love and 'in love' was still there; ready to entrap them if they ever got a chance to be alone again together.

9

The ultra modern and rather sterile Avon board-meeting room was large and stuffed with high-tech gadgets for power meetings and presentations to the senior management of our client.

"Not what you'd expect from an old and long established bank like Barclays is it?" Barry expressed in disdain.

"I mean, look at all this crappy shiny chrome and whatnots everywhere. What happened to good ol' polished grainy wood wall panels and classy stud-fastened leather upholstery eh? " He continued.

"Pass me the memory stick and stop grumbling like an old man" I said, taking the flash memory stick and plugging it in the laptop. "You did remember to save the latest presentation file on the stick didn't you?" Barry nodded still surveying the large meeting room decor with disgust barely disguised.

"If we pull this off today I bet you won't give a damn what your ass touches in their boardroom at the next meeting when they give us the deal. Whether leather, chrome or plain old plastic; right?"

He chuckled and rubbed his palms together gleefully.

"I'm already imagining sitting in the 50 degrees sun of the desert, me legs knee deep in blue sea water."

"Can't be that hot, and if the sea was that blue you be more than knee deep in the sea you twat! Anyway, Dubai isn't the desert it used to be from what I've heard" I pointed out, referring to my brief online research on the rapidly developing Arab city.

"Nah, you're wrong there mate, I saw the weather report on TV last night on that place, bloody 45 degrees already. Can you believe that?

"To be honest; no I can't" I replied genuinely surprised. As Barry and I fiddled with the awkward presentation projector, Jemma strode towards us where we were busy setting up the presentation. I looked up as she crossed the room from the corner where she had been chit-chatting with two of the client's executive directors. They were all smiles as their gaze followed almost rhythmically, Jemma's exaggerated hip swings. They reminded me of the Goofy cartoon character watching a tasty bone swinging right in front of him, eyes-popping, tongue trawling the floor salivating like a rabid hound. She had them almost where she wanted them; she knew it and they were yet to discover it, whenever they reached consciousness.

Not only is she smart and keeps up well with techie sales support guys like Barry but she brings a whole new meaning to the terms 'customer driven' and 'customer satisfaction'. She has Hellenic stature and features, goddess-like long, dark, curly hair and a body to die for and still made you wish there is an after-life. Once with her could never be enough. She used all she had to get the deals and that's why she's constantly our top sales performer.

We worked well together, I find them and prep them, she takes over to keep their interest and finally to get the deal. Barry supported us technically and together, we formed a sales attack cell that's been the most successful across all the regions covered by the company.

Today was our chance for a last pitch before the bank's Europe, Middle-East and Africa board. A decision as to which agent will get the marketing and branding contract for opening the Dubai market for them was expected within days.

Dubai had been perceptively expanding and modernising at breakneck speed for 5-6 years or so now. The property market growth in particular was showing incredible investment gains. The whole cauldron was fired by one of, if not the largest construction exercise in the world. Demand for mortgages was running high but Barclays had decided to wait before entering the market. They wanted to see if the Dubai property market boom would be popped by the federal government of the United Arab Emirates of which Dubai was one of the seven emirates or states. To add to the bank's hesitation, there were market rumours the federal government; seated in the official capital Abu Dhabi would not allow the continued sale of houses which included land. This was something of a definite 'no-no' in the minds of the power custodians that sat in Abu Dhabi

"Gentlemen, are you all set?" Jemma enquired as she reached us. "The vice-president is delayed in another meeting. He'll join us shortly; we now have 5 directors including the technical director and head of operations so let's get started."

Barry frowned as I gave him a knowing look; we both expected what came next.

"Let's start with the technical presentation and slip the executive overview for when the VP comes in. Barry?" she continued.

Wordless, he nodded and flipped the order of the presentation slides as Jemma calmly introduced the topic and agenda. Reminding the audience of the need to make a decision sooner than later since they already 'almost missed the boat' in Dubai.

Barry was ready to present the technical slides by the time Jemma finished her introduction and pep talk.

We knew it was 'do or die' as I gave Barry a covert 'thumbs up' to encourage him whilst Jemma took her seat next to me.

It wasn't a done deal by any means, even with Jemma in our camp. We were under strong competitive pressure not just from our traditional rivals here but also from Indian and Lebanese companies partnering with local Arab companies based in Dubai. We too had partners there of course but the race was truly on.

Barry started hesitantly, speaking louder than he needed to and pacing more than he should. I secretly gave him the 'calm down and slow down' signal we had devised to help each other during customer presentations. He got it and I sensed Jemma's sigh of relief.

***

Almost 5 weeks later, and true to his words, Barry sat in the midday desert sun with his legs in blue water. Not sea water however but we did make it out to Dubai. It was a 'site survey' you might call it; a kind of reconnaissance in preparation for executing the contract which we anticipated from Barclays.

Jemma had received an LOI or Letter of Intent from her client 3 weeks after our presentation. She had played the game well it seemed including ensuring we were the last to present out of the short-listed bidders for the deal. She knew that would give us a crucial advantage due to her intimate knowledge of the executive board of tongue-droppers. Now I used the word 'intimate' on purpose and we'll leave it at that for now.

Barry got his blue water albeit swimming pool blue water at the beach-front hotel. The view of the sea was panoramic. Even the outline of the hotel was something unordinary. Shaped like a gentle sea wave with all windows facing the sea and a nautical theme to many aspects of the rooms and interior, it was a magnificent place to stay for 3 weeks! Some of the outbuildings like restaurants and the conference hall were also built with nautically inspired shapes such as the row-boat form taken by the large detached conference hall.

The view from our room on the 15th floor rivaled the thrilling ride up the see-through elevator. After checking in, we had got in to the ordinary looking lift. Imagine the surprise on our face as we rose past the ground level. It sneakily revealed the awesome landscaped hotel gardens. Then one noticed with a suppressed gasp of pleasure, the backdrop of the blue-tinged yet clear warm Arabian Sea. So close we could almost reach out across the gardens and skim the water with our finger tips as the elevator smoothly took us higher, closer to our floor.

Once in my plush room, my attention was drawn to the floor to ceiling widow show-casing the unobstructed and inviting sea view. I threw my hand luggage on the bed and stepped to the window for a better view. I was suddenly overwhelmed by a feeling of wanting to jump! Vertigo at heights has never been something I could conquer.

I later joined the others downstairs, by the pool. Palm trees swayed in the sea breeze and we sipped cocktails to a toast by Jemma.

"Here's to a job brilliantly done and to our incredible luck!"

"Yes and ably assisted by the incredible bulk!" I joked raising my glass to Barry's large and chubby frame still sat at the pool's edge, splashing the water with his toes.

"Ha-bloody-ha!" he retorted sarcastically.

"You can bank on that too! Barclays Bank? Bank; Get it? He

replied and chuckled. We all laughed out loud and other guests around the bar must have wondered if the heat or the drinks had gone straight to our heads. We didn't care. That's the advantage of being a foreigner.

Later in the evening, I was in the shower when the hotel phone rang. I drew back the shower unit sliding doors and reached for the phone conveniently hung-on the wall close-by.

"Allo?" A voice enquired at the other end of the line.

"Yes can I help you?"

"How are you" she continued in heavily accented English. Her voice was alluring.

"I'm ok thanks!" I replied pleasantly, perhaps a little too excitedly as I wondered if I got lucky with an Arabian girl on my first day out here! I assumed she was a hotel guest either bored or had seen us earlier and tracked me down or just called the wrong number but decided to get friendly. Either way, whatever way, I encouraged her.

"What about yourself? Where're you from?" I asked.

"From Libanon, you know Libanon?"

"You mean Lebanon? Yes I know of it but never been there"

"Are you here at the hotel alone?" she asked with ease, rolling the 'r' profoundly as Arabs tended to. Something I learned from Edgeware Road in central London which had now been completely taken over by Arab business, mostly restaurants and convenience stores.

How else could I answer such an inviting question?

"Yes, I am. How did you know?" I flirted. She giggled and asked;

"Do you want a girlfriend? Wait a moment"

'Do I want a girlfriend?' I wasn't expecting things to work out that fast. I waited: paused my answer until her return.

"Hallo, how long you will stay here?" This time it was a man's voice, the English was clearer but it sounded like the same accent. 'Perhaps he's her brother and is helping her because he speaks slightly better English'. I thought, trying to convince myself away from the darker reality that was forming in my head.

"I'm not sure as yet" I answered cautiously.

"Okay; don't worry, tell me. How many nights you want? How

much you can pay?

And there it was!

***

"Ha ha ha!" Barry guffawed. Unable to control himself from laughing at my expense as I recited the experience to him later that evening as we sat in the lounge of the night-club that was part of our hotel.

"You mean you almost got yourself a nice local hooker and you're in the country less than a couple of hours!" He continued, having a field day of it. "Whatever shall I tell Rosemary?"

"Don't you dare breathe a word of it to her!" I cautioned unconvincingly.

"What's it worth for me to keep my mouth shut tight then? That's gonna cost you at least a couple of pints!"

"Yeah go on then" I said, resigned to give in to Barry's mock blackmail.

"I see 'She who must be adored' Jemma's having a good laugh out there on the dance floor."

We could just about make out her tall outline as she danced a millimeter away from the general manager of our local agent.

Though she tried her best to maintain that distance, his sporadic jerky movement which he clearly considered as a dance form must have been physically painful for Jemma. Oblivious to the music tempo, he bumped his knee, elbow and possibly his chin against her with arms flailing reminding me of fleeing Japanese movie characters as Godzilla approached. Except he gesticulated, rooted to the spot.

"May the gods of music forgive him, I know I can't. That's a Michael Jackson classic they're playing for crissake!" I protested loudly. Barry laughed and in his inimitable tactless style, mimicked the arm thrashing of Jemma's rhythm-challenged dance partner. I couldn't help but laugh at Barry's antics. He was always a good laugh even at times when others might consider I've gone too far with my teasing of him. If I can't have fun and take the piss out of my best mate, who else can I do so with? I thought, justifying to myself.

"Guess what?"

"What?" Jemma replied Barry as she returned to our table with

Khalifah the dancer close behind. I gave her a quick visual medical check-over to make sure she was none-the-worse for the abuse she'd suffered on the dance floor. She seemed ok.

"What?" She repeated as Barry had momentarily forgotten to disclose whatever tantalising information he had up his sleeves. He was distracted. A sexily and expensively dressed small group of three Arabic looking girls with 'come and talk to me if you dare' looks, walked closely past us. Actually, past poor old Barry, with their combined perfume power wafting right up his nostrils. I knew it was strong because they passed further away from me and I had to stop breathing temporarily in order to survive. They were gorgeous and poor Barry must have taken the full brunt of the aromatic attack.

"Tobi's already found himself a girl, an Arabic one too. He's gone local and he's hardly been here a day! I reckon he's done alright! Eh mate?" He finally responded to Jemma's repeated question, giving me a wink and a dig with his elbow.

"Go on tell 'em' He continued. "Or shall I?"

"Be my guest" I invited.

It was embarrassing that I thought I got lucky so fast but what the heck. Anyway, something deeper worried me, I had a girlfriend, a nice one too, and I have a lover that I still couldn't get over. Yet, I was readily aroused by an anonymous albeit tantalising phone call. Do I even know what I want anymore? Perhaps it's the nature of man to forever be the hunter. And perhaps the interest wanes once the 'kill' is made'. I sincerely hoped not, not with Carlene. It was different; it just has to be different. I've looked forward to somehow finding her again but the reality is the more I've tried, the further I realised that I am away from that goal. The Internet had been a distraction rather than helping. I certainly found no lead to track Carlene down and the Net was crawling with people that had issues, that much was clear. It's not a crowd I wanted to be in.

"...can you believe he actually bought it; or I should say, he almost bought her!" The others laughed as Barry reached the climax of his tale.

"Actually, this is becoming very common here in the UAE now. Especially in Dubai unfortunately" Khalifah informed the group. We nodded in acceptance of his words. After all, as a 'local', a national of the UAE, he should know.

Yet, I had to ask the question although as part of our brief before coming out here, we had been strongly advised to avoid discussions relating to sensitive issues. Religion was one of those issues.

"I have to admit Mr. Khalifah, I was rather surprised that something like that can happen in a 5-star hotel in an Islamic country. And from what you just said, it wasn't an isolated incident."

"Yes of course; you are right. But you have to remember, Dubai is positioning itself as a truly international and modern city of the 21st century. You will see the successes. Dubai is probably the fastest growing city in the world and the construction projects are extensive, on massive scales at neck-break speed; sorry, break-neck speed"

"Dubai hosts many international events from sports to culture and trade. Can you believe that 80% of Dubai's inhabitants are foreigners?!" He continued. We didn't dare to stop him; probably more from the informative content than business etiquette.

"Even our airline, Emirates, has won many international awards not to mention the world's only 7-star hotel is here in Dubai. But you know, there are negative sides to these achievements and we pray to Allah that we can manage them." His pleasant elocution was a sharp contrast to his dance floor skills clearly.

"Prostitution seems to be a necessary evil due to man's nature. We have many, many, many single men working here as labourers and so on. We also suffer from high road accident rates; the city perhaps is too busy, hectic even"

This led us then to open the discussion around why we were in Dubai. To understand what made the city and the country in general tick so we can exploit these unique traits in introducing and establishing Barclays' presence in this renascent Arabian country.

We had decided to return to England a week early as our initial work had been completed faster than expected. Two days before our departure from the hotel, I received a text message on my mobile. The number wasn't familiar, neither was the country code at first. Then it dawned on me. It was from here. Here being the UAE.

The message was from a Suchada Koyama. Just simply

apologising for contacting me late and asking for a call back when I'm free. Suchada; I wondered, yes of course! We had met on the Emirates Airlines flight here from Heathrow airport.

Suchada Koyama worked for Emirates Airlines, although she had been on the flight as a regular passenger.

We sat next to each other and I did not know she was a cabin crew member until I noticed she exchanged greetings and glances a lot with the flight cabin crew.

She later explained, as her colleagues served lunch that she was flying back to her base in Dubai after a holiday in England to visit her friends there.

The flight had been fully booked and we had not been able to confirm a business-class seat but we wanted to show our potential client that we were fast acting and ready to commit to their needs. So we had opted for economy-class seats. We didn't even have the option to sit together.

My chat with Suchada certainly compensated for the reduced in-flight comfort of the economy or 'cattle-class' seats as Barry was fond of saying.

I had completely forgotten I gave her my business card and had asked her to contact me whilst I was in Dubai. She was also based there as she explained; Dubai is the hub for Emirates Airlines operations and the vast majority of the airline's flight crew were based there.

***

I called her and we met later in the morning after further teasing and tormenting by Barry and a promise to buy him more beer when we got back to London.

As she still had some days remaining from her leave, we spent most of the day and evening together and she seemed very pleased to give me a tour of Dubai. To be honest while the city was impressive in the terms described by Khalifah, I was unable to get a feeling of 'soul' in the city. That didn't matter however, we enjoyed the bumps and jostling in the 4-wheel-drive car that took us on the popular 'desert safari' rides on the huge sand dunes in the desert. And in the evening, as part of the tour the organisers had laid out a pseudo desert camp where we took a very short ride on the obliging but forever slobbering camels. The tricky part was getting up and down. I expect the women enjoy the rocking, sensuous motion of the camels' back once they finally got up there. The men had to watch out for the hump that threatened to castrate or at least, debilitate the unwary when it was time to get down as the camel lowered its forelegs first rather jerkily.

The on-the-spot barbecue; prepared by the drivers was delicious. We ate sumptuously as we sat cross-legged on cushions arranged around a floor stage where a belly-dancer twirled to the sultry Arabian music under a moon and stars that promised to always be there.

It was romantic, it was alluring and to surrender to the ambience seemed the only option one could have.

Discourteously, but unintentionally, I thought 'where are you Carlene, why can't this be you, here now?'

Prompted by a grab on her arms, and encouraged by my gentle push on her back, Suchada got up to dance with the entertainer who was still going around the edge of the stage encouraging others to get up and dance too. I watched them all dance and noted that Mr. Khalifah had some serious competition here. The pumping music seemed to elicit the weirdest 'dance' motions from the tourists on the stage but I must have been the only one that was noticing. I caught a glimpse of Suchada doing her best to the music and I got up and joined her and wondered what others thought about my rusty robotic dance.

Judging by Suchada's feigned expression of embarrassment, I was destined to join the hall of infamy along with the great Mr. Khalifah!

I looked at Suchada as I dropped her off by taxi at her place in one of the many residential towers occupied by Emirates Airlines staff. Her shared apartment was on the 33rd floor of a shiny new building that lined the most famous road in Dubai. Along it were the country's plushest residential and office towers along with major international group hotels including Shangri La, Crowne Plaza, Dusit (a major Thai hotel group) and Fairmont.

As she walked away towards the building entrance, I knew she would be too much to forget; all at once. We clearly felt a strong connection despite her typical Asian shyness. I admired her elegance, graciousness and humility and what an absolute stunner in the looks department!

Women like that don't 'grow' every day in England I thought, perhaps not in Europe too. She made me realise that Asia truly was full of promise. My Eastern promise was who? Carlene? Suchada? Or?

I once read somewhere that if the gods wished to punish you, they would grant your wish but in a multitude so you would have to make a decision.

As if to crystallize this prophecy, my next destination would take me right where I had not expected at all. There, just 2 months later, I would also discover just how fragile our tenure on life truly is.

10

Tobi yawned and stretched luxuriously as he gazed across the large aqua-marine pool that ran almost blending with the sea that swayed back and forth ahead of him. The Dusit Hotel and Polo Resort in Hua Hin, Thailand was definitely a place which demands that you relax in as gentle a manner as you can imagine. Taking a break from the hectic promotional schedule for his novel, Carlene, his publisher had invited him to the resort away from the busier promotional venue, Dusit Hotel in Bangkok.

His novel Carlene had been on the book shelves in the West for almost a year. Writing the book had been some kind of releasing experience for him he summarised.

***

I was even thinking less and less of Carlene. The guilt I felt about keeping Rosemary on the shelf for so long had been too strong and finally I decided to 'come clean' shortly after publishing my novel, Carlene. There had been no point in perpetuating the charade. She had been and probably still is very upset and I absolutely cannot blame her. She deserved better and she got better. At least for her, she and my best friend, The Pooh, hooked up well and are very close from what I hear.

Barry and I had talked about it of course and I told him to go for it and meant it. Barry's a great guy and I knew for all his other faults, he would be good for her. But I decided to keep some distance for a while it would be too much to deal with parting with Rosemary and still seeing her everyday with my best friend.

Yes I know it was all amicable but, still too much to deal with for all. We thought maybe later when they were settled into each other and I had time to get used to it all, we could get back and be best of pals again.

My publisher had decided to premier the Asia publishing of Carlene at Dusit Hotel in Bangkok, Thailand. The novel had been generally well received by the critics although one or two did give rather skewed reviews that mystified me and no doubt those that matter most, the readers.

It was as we laid back in the deck chairs by the pool that I received the first phone call. It was my youngest brother Deji.

"Hi Deji: how's little bro?" I answered; recognising his number.

"Tobi, dad's not well. He's been in hospital for the past three days. He didn't tell anyone until we found out yesterday. He said he thought it wasn't anything serious and you know him, he didn't want to worry us".

I was stunned for a moment. My father was not a sickly type of person although he had a problem with conjunctivitis in his eyes but at his age of 53 it's not so grave.

He had only just turned 53 yesterday. I had not been able to reach him on the phone and had to leave a message on the answering machine. That would explain why, he had admitted himself at the hospital.

"What's wrong with dad, what is he ill from?!"

"Hepatitis C has been diagnosed" Deji said, gravely.

"Where are you now Deji? At the hospital?", I asked trying to stay calm but my head was throbbing and my heart quickened as I tried to make sense of this insane and sudden turn of event.

"Yes but dad's asleep now, we didn't call you yesterday because he seemed fine and decided to call you later. He's in a critical state Tobi.

You better fly back" The tone of my brother's voice reverberated through me. He was clearly very serious and very worried. I thought, how brave he was, to make this call. How brave my other brother Tunji and my sister Demi also were to be dealing with this family tragedy and I am out here in the glorious but now irrelevant scenery.

My mother was also not in England, she and Dad had only

recently planned their return from Lagos back to England having gone back home to Nigeria for some years once we were settled in England.

Dad returned first having retired first. He was preparing the home and the way for mum's return due less than 8 months away following her own retirement from her job in Nigeria.

England was our family home and we all had hoped to be together there now that our parents would retire.

"Have you told mum?" I asked although I knew the answer.

"Yes of course, Tunji called her just now. She plans to fly out with the first flight possible"

"Ok, stay calm bro' ok? I'll also get the first flight I can back to England and I'll let you all know. Don't leave his side alright?" I said, unnecessarily. Our family is extremely supportive of each other and we dearly love and respect our parents.

I was torn apart with worry and it was only with the help of my publishing agent and Suchada's typical Thai calmness that I made it back to Bangkok in less than 3 hours.

***

Both Dusit hotels had been unable to get me a flight leaving earlier than another 2 days due to the busy travel month of December.

It was an agonising night that I spent at the hotel in Bangkok. Suchada was the pillar that held me up as she stayed with me.

I was woken up somewhere in the middle of the night by a phone call from Deji. My father had passed away. I was devastated, my heart wrenched apart and I cried the first tears that I remember since the break with Carlene.

But these tears came from somewhere beyond my body, forming a reservoir behind my eyes, building up pressure. Why him? Why now? How can he be gone? I just left a birthday voice greeting for him 2 days ago on his answering machine where I heard his voice prompting to leave a message. Why am I stuck so far away now?

I did not want to control myself anymore, why can't a man cry. And I did, as Suchada did all she could to console me and to try to calm my body that convulsed sympathetically with the tears that came from so deep that it could only have meant my soul was awash with sorrow and grief at the loss of my father. I could not speak to him to be there to comfort him and share the responsibility with my ever-so-brave siblings. How pitiful can it get? Yet it got worse that my mother was also unable to get a flight out in time to be at the deathbed of her sick and dying beloved husband she had known since the age of 17. They were so close to their dream of retirement and a life of peace in the vicinity of their children in England.

Who does one have to blame? It seems someone must be blamed for something that shouldn't have happened. Why was the diagnosis not reached earlier, so that effective treatment could be administered? Was there effective treatment? Were the doctors diligent in their duty? Should we have somehow known earlier? Why was he able to be in the hospital alone for two days before we found out? Why did God take this man who was a true man of God in practice?

It was not a time for laying blame. Rather, it was time to show support and strength for the whole family. Especially for my poor mother, the only man she has known her whole adult life, suddenly gone with less than a day's warning and she, separated by distance she could not cover in time.

Both my mother and I arrived home in London the day after my dad had passed away. She arrived from Lagos and I from Bangkok.

***

My two brothers and cousin Dotun and I conducted the cleansing of my father's body after the embalming at the funeral parlour.

Afterwards, we agreed on distributed duties. I was to return to the hospital where dad had passed away to claim and collect the rest of his personal belongings and documentation needed for his death certificate.

Finding a parking spot at the hospital was not an easy task and after several turns around the car park I finally managed to squeeze into a free space.

I returned to the car with the belongings of my father and tears welled up in my eyes again, something which we had all experienced on and off since dad's passing. It just started anytime, anywhere, triggered by a memory or feeling of remorse sometimes of guilt without origin or reason.

I reversed out of the parking spot perhaps a little more abruptly than I should have and almost knocked a doctor down as she passed behind my car.

I got out to apologise as I realised I had been rather careless and she had dropped her bag at the scare.

I picked up her bag and I handed it to her and was about to say sorry when I saw the cute grin that was so familiar and so missed over so many years.

"Tobi! How are you?! What are you doing here, at the hospital?!" Carlene spoke with such surprise and delight.

"What am I doing here?! What are you doing here in England?! You're supposed to be in America or Malaysia!" I couldn't hide my joy at seeing her after all the years I'd schemed ways to at least meet her again, now here I was, meeting her totally by accident. Yes, literally almost by an accident!

I told her about my father's passing away. She was clearly moved as she knew him and they both got on very well. In fact after my break up with Carlene, dad had given me council. He had told me that he doubted I would ever find a better girl and had guided me on how to be a 'man' in such situation in the future. I learned that well from him.

She enquired about my mother and how she was bearing up and my brothers and sister. She told me she was separated from her husband and had moved to England some months ago. She was now working at the hospital and regretted she had not contacted me earlier as she would have wanted to check on my father during his stay at the hospital.

I expressed my regret that her marriage was ending and asked about Megan.

"She's staying with her grand parents in Dakota right now and I plan to go and get her in a few months once I establish myself here and stabilise." She replied.

She asked about the funeral arrangement details. We exchanged contact numbers and agreed to meet for coffee and bring each other up to date on over 10 years of separation.

11

The funeral had been a heart-wrenching, soul destroying experience. Carlene knew the man she had once loved so wholly would never be able to fully recover from the loss of his father. She too had been so intensely moved by the closeness of Tobi's family as they struggled to somehow deal with their sorrow and conduct the last rites for the much loved head of their family.

She too had felt warmth from Tobi's father and mother. They had welcomed her so easily into their family. That they liked her so much was evident during her first weekend stay with them in London. She liked the family very much including Tobi's siblings, especially his sister Demi, so cute and effeminate despite growing up with three brothers.

A vision of Tobi's father's kind and cheerful face stayed with her as she gave a silent moment's thought for him.

'May his soul rest in everlasting peace' she prayed.

Tobi's father had also, in the workings of fate, played a major part in bring her and his son back together and she was forever grateful to him. She also wondered if she should ironically, be grateful to Lemon also. After all, it was his gift that had inadvertently given Carlene the hope of finding Tobi again. Of course she had no way of knowing what status she would find Tobi in, if ever she did find him. She was married so why would she not expect him to also have a family by now?

Although they had been unable to keep their appointment a week after being miraculously reunited, Carlene felt exhilaration equaled only by a previous encounter.

It had been with the same man, at the first meeting years ago but it took only moments to recover the emotions of that time.

She guiltily considered that despite electing to be with Bob, whom she truly had loved and perhaps still love, the passion had never reached quite the same level as with Tobi.

Guilty because of the sense of duty she felt to her husband whom she has been separated from for almost 13 months now. But also guilt for leaving the man she knew desperately loved her but was too young to help her do what she knew she had to do.

Her mother had always told her that love cannot solve everything but it can sweeten everything. She knew she had to settle down and take the burden off her mother who had taken up the challenge of supporting the family when her ailing father was no longer able to do so.

Carlene sat up in the bed, turned on the bedside light and reached without needing to look, for the book she knew was always there, beside her.

She read the back cover again, for the umpteenth time. Her mind drifted, effortlessly on winds of thought blowing here and there in distant corners where she had kept her secret love hidden for ever so long.

His face appeared, clear as day though the night prevailed outside. It seemed he had hardly changed from the boy of 19. She laughed silently as she remembered his comical attempt to boost his age from 19 across the monumental gap to the age of 20. Just so he could be closer to her age-wise at their first meeting. There's something about spring that always brought a sense of hope for her, not only the fact that her birthday occurred in that season. And true enough, she'd had lighter feet as she had stepped unto the train followed by her cousin. She had also been worried. She looked forward to her first days of training at Black Notley Hospital with trepidation. Then she met Tobi. The sensations of love and in-love carried her through the most difficult part of the whole training experience.

Being in such a small town, one might even say, village, far away from family and long-known friends, was no longer so emotionally arduous. She always had Tobi and she was his. From the first day it had been like they grew up together, been the closest of friends. She had always felt the more mature with Tobi though. That had always burned at her subconsciously. Years later now, she realised her folly of giving up a love so deep and natural for a dream that was not really hers but rather, her mother's dream for her daughter.

The day Tobi came to her dormitory, with all those memories expressed in letters and cards and photos, she had seen him pull up in his car. Not far from below her bay window.

The car, she had not recognised but the young man that stepped out and looked up towards her window, she knew and loved like no other before.

The tricks of light had let her see him but he clearly could not see her as she watched him hesitate with one leg out of the car. Waiting, for what, she didn't know at the time. Then he finally came out and his next appearance at her door brought an official end to her greatest love. One that she had triggered an end to: during moments of cold-calculation.

After he had left that day, she locked herself in her room for three days, refusing to answer phone calls. She ignored even knocks on the door by her colleagues and friends at the hospital except to tell the more persistent ones to leave her alone. She definitely did not want to talk to Bob of all people and for those three days she blocked him out of her mind as best she could. He was to blame. Why did he have to come between Tobi and her, with an offer she could not ignore at a time when she had been feeling pressure to decide her future.

She called in sick and risked failing her tests but why would she care anymore? Her mind and heart just wasn't strong enough for it.

She heard of Tobi's calls too but she knew what would happen if she heard his voice. She already knew how he was feeling. If they talked now, she would give up the dream to be settled quickly and Bob had laid that chance at her feet.

Crying herself to sleep at night and gazing at the tranquil scenery from her window in the day, she cried.

Sitting here now, in her bed, 10 years on, she cried at the loss of love and sheer unbridled happiness she had shared with Tobi then. Perhaps her love, her true love, could once again be hers and she swore to herself never to push it away or let it slip out of her life again

12

Hemmed in by the crowd, Tobi walked up the stairs in a slight zigzag manner in order to avoid the would-be underground train passengers rushing downstairs towards the platform. They hoped to catch the train that just squeezed him and his fellow passengers out moments earlier before it departed again.

Emerging into the bright Spring Sunday light at Bayswater Underground Station, he turned left and headed towards one of his favourite mall hangouts in London.

As with the rest of the family, the past 3 weeks since Tobi's dad's funeral had been quite draining for him. As they say, 'life must go on' and that is what he had used to drive himself on, to be strong for the family. He was now the new male head of the family with responsibilities he hadn't expected to have to carry so soon. Yet, that is what he must do.

Having been too preoccupied with issues related to his dad's funeral and his job, he had simply ran out of time to meet Carlene as they had planned. Their only meeting following the near-accident at the hospital car-park was at the funeral. She had been incredibly supportive and seemed to fit is so rapidly with the family, like a family member in fact. To him, she actually looks better with age. Some women have it and some don't it seems; that illusive ability to look better with age. Perhaps it really is true that beauty is in the eye of the beholder.

"Good afternoon sir, can I help you? A table for how many sir?" The waitress had asked in a professionally polite manner.

"A table for two please: thank you" Tobi replied "Oh by the

fountain would be fine. Cheers"

He was excited, eager to see Carlene again. He wondered at the possibility of them getting back together and just as quickly dismissed the thought. 'She's married for goodness sake!' he reminded himself miserably. Deep in his thoughts, he heard the echo of a distant mobile phone ringing. He reached for his mobile but it wasn't his that had been called. He looked to his right, at the Chinese couple sat at the table on the other side of the miniature fountain. The girl had answered her phone and was speaking in 'Chinglish' He supposed one might call it. Mixing her Chinese with English every so often, she seemed engrossed.

He remember Carlene had once advised him on how to find a good Chinese restaurant;

"You should eat where you see plenty of Chinese eating…" she had said. It seemed logical enough so here he was; at Spoons Chinese restaurant in Whiteley's shopping mall waiting for his once-upon-a-time love long separated by time and changes to both their lives.

"… a bomb scare in the tube? …oh my god … are you alright dad? The desperate concern and shock was evident in the girl's voice as she talked on her mobile.

Tobi was alarmed too. He now worried about Carlene, his family; friends and colleagues some of whom he was sure would be traveling on the underground. The girl had asked one of the waiters to switch the television to a news channel which was covering the scare. At least it seems like that's all it was, a scare.

Why hadn't Carlene called? He thought.

"After the devastating series of terror bomb attacks on the London's public transport barely a year ago where almost 50 people were killed, it's no wonder people were jittery about this alarm.." the news reporter was saying on the now blaring TV which had drawn everyone's attention in the restaurant.

Tobi tried to call Carlene and received a number unobtainable error message back. He turned to the news screen again and consternation furrowed his forehead. As he was about to try her number again, the phone rang, this time it was his phone. It was his mother, calling to check that he was ok as she knew he be out today to meet Carlene. He asked about his siblings and his mum confirmed they'd called to say they were fine. Ordinarily he would have driven into London and would have picked Carlene up by car. But it was such a lovely spring day and London has been almost turned into a no-go area for private cars at certain times. Apart from meeting for lunch, they had made no other plans except to take it as it came. It was just better to do all the traveling by the 'tube', London's underground train system and the buses.

Then he saw her striding energetically towards their table as she immediately recognised him of course.

"Hey Tobi; I'm so sorry! The trains were delayed and my phone battery died on me. I had no way to…" I got up and hugged her for goodness knows how long. I kissed her forehead like a father would; such was my relief that I hardly heard her pleading voice.

"Tobi, are you ok, you're crushing me, Tobi…"

"Oh sorry Carlene, I'd just been afraid that something might have happened to you." Only the couple at the table next to us would have understood why I nearly suffocated the life out of her in gratitude to the gods that be. Contradictory perhaps but isn't love; in many ways?

"Why? What were you afraid of?" she asked.

"You don't know?

"Know what? Are you winding me up TV?" she said playfully.

"About the bomb scare in the tube just now; well, an hour or so ago" I informed her.

"No, I didn't, you're serious aren't you?" I nodded and turned her gaze with mine, towards the news report that was still playing but now at a much reduced volume. Almost echoing the lowering of the nationwide state of worry somewhat.

"Oh my, thank God it seems to have been only a scare!" she said, as the much more dangerous alternative to situation dawned on her.

I motioned her to sit down and I sat opposite. I watched her as she placed her bag on the free seat next to her. I remembered there was a time she would have insisted on me sitting next to her or vice versa, never opposite if the choice was there. We even called ourselves by name, in discretion; endearments were left out of the conversation. So much water had passed under the proverbial bridge and there was a lot to catch up on. Our lives had been changed in many ways.

We smiled awkwardly to each other and the waitress saved us as her offered us the menu.

"It's so good to see you Carlene. "

"I'm so happy to see you too!"

We talked lightly about so many things that sitting in a restaurant would allow yet our feelings ran deeper than the words were allowed to express in such a public place. But we knew.

***

The closest gate to Hyde Park was only a short walk from Whiteley's and the warm air and bright skies of April's end encouraged a leisurely walk.

We brushed hands as we waited at the kerb, for the traffic lights to halt the flow of vehicles and give way to the flow of humanity, some with their pet in-tow.

On the other side of the road, I was about to guide Carlene through the open wrought iron gates of the great park when, on impulse, I took her hand and change direction. I wanted to show her something first.

We walked along the narrow pavement of Bayswater Road just outside the park's fencing. Lined along the rails of the fence and partly on the ground close to the fence were an eclectic collection of artwork of all forms one could imagine. Each Sunday, this section of Bayswater Road was turned into a long and narrow arts bazaar where amateur artists could display and sell the results of their efforts. Be it pottery, oil paintings, figures made out of clock parts, wood carvings or whatsoever, you could find it here sometimes at a reasonable price too.

There was a 15 inch by 15 inch oil painting, elegantly framed that caught Carlene's eye. She said it reminded her somehow, of how she had dreamt her home in the USA would be. It was a white-washed villa on a cliff directly overlooking a beautiful blue sea. It somehow reminded me of the villas in Greece, standing proud and strong with an amazing sea view.

I bought the painting for Carlene and gifted it to her for her birthday which I had missed as it had been just after my father's funeral.

She thanked me and gave me a hug, such a familiar and much-missed hug. It was all I could do to stop myself from turning that hug into an everlasting kiss.

We entered the park from the next gate we arrived at.

"I missed this place so much TV, it's really so good to be here with you again. This was our place right? Our special place"

I squeezed her hand in silent response.

"This will be the first special place I'll bring Megan to when she comes". That pleased me more than she could have imagined.

"You miss her don't you?" I asked without need

"Yes, very much but we talk often on the phone and she's doing fine at school grandma Jo' tells me" she replied then fell loudly silent.

"Are you ok honey?" I enquired, letting slip an endearment that escaped my guard.

"I was just wondering how it would have been, if you and I had had Megan. I was thinking how we would be now, taking this walk, in this park, the three of us"

We walked along the bank of willow trees and stopped to play with the ever-so inquisitive yet nervous grey squirrels of the park. They snatched tidbits we offered them then skipped away with their typical jerky, nervous movements.

We sat at the bank of the pond, covered by the protecting droopy leaves and branches of the willows. We watched the ducks dart around on the pond in search of tasty water-borne morsels. They were noticeably being careful not to disturb their neighbours, the cantankerous geese and the sedate but equally unforgiving swans.

I'd always liked Kenneth Grahame's The Wind In The Willows. Perhaps that's why the willow tree holds such a special place in my heart. Next to me now sat someone who had never left my heart. Though we had lost each other for a long while, we could talk like we only skipped a day.

"Honey, I'm so sorry that I was so immature at a time when you needed me to be a real man. At least to give you a plan for our future together; instead I acted like a jerk, a real twat. I know now. I knew the moment I left your place that day" It had taken a decade to get those words out of my mind, face-to-face with Carlene. What an incredible release I felt after.

Carlene was silent, I turned to her again. Her tears fell in slow, tantalising trickles down her cheeks. As a grown man, I now know the importance of letting the tears fall and run their course. I saw it as the body cleansing its soul of poisonous, trapped emotions.

I gently pulled her head to my shoulders and held her there by an arm across her shoulder that was now heaving as she sobbed softly, almost privately.

From my own experience the day we finally said goodbye that hundreds of words lay behind those tears. Words of regret, despair, sadness at making the wrong decisions and finding oneself at the painful end of ones own mistakes. But I also felt these were tears of hope and gratefulness for a second chance. At least, I hope I'm right in thinking that.

"Tobi can you ever forgive me, I can't tell you how much I thought about you through the years. Even on our wedding day, I looked at Bob and I saw you. I had to force myself to stop or I would have gone crazy really. "

"I know what I did was bad, it was wrong for our love. You needed more time; I was letting myself fall under pressure. I'd wanted to live a dream that wasn't mine when all along I should have waited for you. I know how it must have hurt you" she continued as I listened, barely able to control the rush of tears that threatened to force their way through.

"I was so happy when I saw your book. Then all at once I was confused. I tried very hard to be a good wife Tobi. Despite you, despite my unchanged love for you; I know it's stupid, wistful and corny but if I could turn back the time, I wouldn't think twice"

"I know honey; I thought the same and did many crazy things to try to find you again, to at least let you know how sorry I was. I didn't want you going through your new life wondering if I was as cold as I acted. It was defensive. I felt incapable of competing with him. I felt inadequate; it seemed it would be easier to let you go than to admit I'd lost you. I should have given you some hope about a future together and planned it with you." I said to her as a tear finally got out and rolled down followed by more.

"Dad was right, but I was stubborn, angry that you would consider Bob over me, Immaturity is all I can blame and myself in general, I actually thought it was materialism that made you want to be with him, since I was just a student and he was traveled and had a real job. Being younger than you didn't help I'm sure." I said in self-reproach.

She giggled as she snuggled closer.

"You were so cute the way you came up and showed me your beautiful car and invited me for a ride in it. I never forgot that"

"Oh so now it's a beautiful car huh? Then you didn't show any interest at all" I said in mock disdain.

"Yep, I actually liked your car and really wanted to ride in it" she said

"So why didn't you accept?"

"I was afraid being with you would make me change my mind darling. I had made a commitment to Bob … it was a mistake, I see that now. I'm just happy we got a second chance to at least be close friends in the same country"

She told me about Mrs. Patterson and Lemon, our inadvertent and luckless cupid as we laid on our back, exchanging life stories of the lost period in our love.

As it turned out, Bob and Satana had not been able to keep away from each other. I told her about Rosemary and Suchada and of course we talked about Carlene, the book.

13

I realized at once that I'd over dressed. I should have known what to expect from the captain's announcement. My second time in Dubai and the heat still caught me by surprise. As the plane's doors were opened and we all trooped out eager to escape into the sunlight, my guess is many were surprised too. If one set an oven for maximum heat for 30 minutes then opened the door and stuck one's head close to the inside, that's the feeling we experienced.

"41 bloody degrees my arse. That captain must've been joking, more like a 100!" Exclaimed Barry as he followed close behind down the aircraft's steps.

Reaching the tarmac I remembered when I was a kid in Lagos and how I used to walk around barefoot. The soles of my feet had hardened in those days and it was like I had built-on leather sandals then. No pain got through. For many years since, my feet have been cocooned in woolen and cotton socks making them overly soft and no longer hardy. I wouldn't dare to walk barefoot here now, I'd out-dance, out-step, out "ooooo" Michael Jackson on my way to the bus waiting to take us to the arrival and transit areas of Dubai International airport.

The loaded bus trundled around the airport and many, new to Dubai wondered at the amount of heavy construction that was clearly taking place on the airport premises. A newer and bigger terminal it seemed and no doubt the marketers of Dubai Inc. are already drooling at the thought of claims they would make proclaiming the airport as setting some record or other. It's the business I'm in and we had returned to the Arabian city to do just that for our client,

Barclays Bank. Jemma had received the contract she'd coveted for so long which now established her as queen of the hill of sales. Barry and I were of course a major part of that success but don't try reminding Jemma and her boss that!

***

We stood in a queue inside the immigration hall, looking around at the mix of travelers.

"So what's it like to be back here then TV?" Barry asked. "It's your chance to hook-up with that hooker friend of yours again isn't it? *Hooker*, hook-up, get it?" he continued the tease.

"Give it up buddy, and don't even think about getting any more free beers out of me for that! Anyway, I'm a free agent now, thanks to you!" I chuckled. "That reminds me, how're you and Rosemary getting on now? It's been quite a few months now".

"Oh, we're alright, she nags every now and then but your loss mate. I should be the one buying *you* free beers. I'm in love and to be perfectly honest with you, I'm planning to propose to her!"

"You're serious?" I asked, somewhat surprised since I had my doubts about the depth that Barry and Rosemary could reach in a relationship. Of course they are two great people but the gap seemed somehow too great to for them to maneuver around. Barry was crass and Rosemary, class. 'Never the twain shall meet' or something like that I thought. But I suppose, as they say - love finds a way – and despite all else, Barry's heart is big and clear. 'A very nice bloke' as the local bargirl at our local pub by the office would say.

"Yeah I'm serious, what do you think of my chance that she'd accept?" he seemed unsure of his standing with Rosemary. I wasn't too surprised about that as Rosemary can be quite an introvert at times.

Like a crowd of penguins with wings clasped to their sides and feet tightly curled around their precious egg, our queue shuffled forward and we followed.

"I mean, I'm head over whatsit in love with her, I don't mind telling you. I think she must love me too, just she never says anything like that. Seems it's not her way like. You know what I mean?"

I nodded in sympathy, understanding his situation well. There had been a time in my relationship with Rosemary that I thought 'what the hell; take the plunge. Carlene's gone; married long time ago and you know that'. I had even scouted for an engagement ring for Rosemary. Love without passion just seemed an inadequate base to build a future on. I needed fire, hot, passionate desire that would make me wake up yearning to see her and would keep my heart going strong until the day's end when I could be with her again. Like a steam engine driven by the burning of coal at its very heart.

I loved Rosemary. Who could not? Her exotic mixed looks, height and grace made her stand out and her sweet demure would be hard to resist. Yet I did resist the final commitment all because of one other who has once again returned. What is not clear still is whether we can belong to each other anew or if what once was can never be again.

***

Suchada was waiting at the meeting point just as she had promised. Her smiling face easily stood out in the clutter of eager faces all seeking to be noticed and acknowledged by those they had come to meet and welcome.

I reached out to hug her then noticed her slight hesitation then I realized it's not something done often in public in this part of the world, and after all, Suchada's also of Thai and Japanese parentage. This no doubt would add to her discretion, her decorum.

Barry nudged me on the arm and I knew exactly what I'd see if I'd turned around, he would be giving me the 'I know what you're up to mate' wink. I ignored him as I didn't want Suchada to feel uncomfortable.

I was very happy to see her again and had actually missed her. She hadn't been able to make the funeral due to her flight roster. But I knew she had wanted nothing else but to be with me to continue the emotional support she had so generously and unexpectedly given me at the moment of getting such bad news about my father's passing.

The fun times we had during my first and last visit to Dubai flashed across my mind. I smiled.

The automatic sliding exit doors opened at our approach and the dense crowd of more people waiting outside to greet arriving passengers was almost overwhelming. It hadn't been too 'in your face' on the previous trip I recalled.

"We must've arrived at a flight rush-hour or something" remarked Barry as we emerged. Had it not been for the temporary steel barriers, forcing a cleared path in a similar manner to how one imagined Jesus parted the Sea of Galilee, we would have been swallowed by the intense crowd. It was a throbbing mix; primarily of South Asians from India, Pakistan and Bangladesh as well as Arabs from near-by Middle-Eastern countries with a noticeable contribution from Asia Pacific, mainly represented by those from the Philippines.

"Yup, you can say that! Actually nowadays it's almost always like this most times of the day and night. Dubai's become very busy especially with manual and semi-skilled labour travelers." Suchada informed.

"Do you enjoy living here then?" Barry directed the question at Suchada as we walked up to yet another queue. This time: at the taxi rank.

"Sometimes I do but I still miss home a lot. I'm just lucky that I can still bid for flights going to Thailand and swap with my colleagues. That way I can get home often to see my friends and family"

"Never been to Thailand, what's it like?" Barry's curiosity continued.

"Well it's very often hot especially during the dry season like around now, but not anything like Dubai though! You should visit my country sometime, I think you'll love it!" she was clearly proud of her country and rightly so from my brief experience.

"You should ask Tobi, he's been there. He can tell you."

"Yes but I was only there for …"

"Oh Tobi I'm so sorry, that was insensitive of me, I didn't mean to – I also wished I could have made it for your dad's funeral. I tried to get a Heathrow or Gatwick flight swap but I couldn't get one in time." She was genuinely upset and apologetic. It was clear. I was surprised as the next moment; she gave me a sideways hug and a lingering peck on the cheek. A taxi pulled up and we were ushered towards it by an Arab taxi queue controller. He was dressed in the national costume of a long white head scarf held in place by a thick rope-like black band and a long white robe which teased the ground from under which a pair of leather sandals could be seen.

The taxi's arrival saved my blushes inspired by Suchada's warm, physical expression of sentiment.

"Where to sir?" asked the smartly uniformed Arab driver. His question was aimed at Barry sitting next to him at the front but he was peering at me and Suchada through his rear-view mirror. I'm not quite sure what the attraction was but a friend of Barry's who used to live in this region, Kuwait I think, had warned him.

As we had sat chatting with him over lunch telling him about our up-coming trip, he'd delivered his advice.

"Let me tell ya' fellows, over in that part of the world, if ya' dropped sumthing, you either bend down and pick it up cautiously; with ya' back to a wall if possible mind ya'. Or; leave the freakin' thing right where it is. You got my meaning like? We all roared in laughter; his broad Northern accent making his quip all the funnier. There was more.

"E'er and don't forget to take a piece of cork with ya', trust me, you'll need it! No, actually, you won't need one Barry; they don't like 'em big and ugly, you'll be alright!" Barry gave him a pretend cuff around the ears as we burst into tear-filled laughter.

Barry was, for the moment anyway, at his best behavior. He'd gone round the back of the car, dumped his luggage into the cavernous taxi's boot and headed straight for the front seat, leaving Suchada and I the back seat.

In the relative privacy of that seat, Suchada had reached out her fingers across the cloth seat and was softly scratching the top of my hand, rested on the seat. I wasn't sure if she was just happy to see me again or something deeper was brewing. If I had to answer that question about myself at that moment, my answer would be an absolute, emphatic 'yes'! The gods had me in punishment, as if in detention at school.

They had answered my prayers of long ago and more recently, all at once in the form of two different women. I could almost see them sat on their thrones or wisps of cloud or whatever, laughing to each other as they waited for my inevitable misery at having to make a decision sooner or later.

Barry was chatting with the driver as best he could in spite of the driver's heavily accented and muddled English diction. It seemed the driver was complaining about the heavy traffic and all too often erratic and dangerous driving in Dubai. It was just what we needed to hear to instill serenity as passengers in his taxi as we zoomed along the freeway. Then the zooming stopped abruptly as we suddenly joined the snail-paced flow of metallic misery that apparently now characterized this hopeful city.

With Suchada at my side and without a business appointment ahead of us for the day, I was relaxed and indulged in conversation with her. Occasionally, Barry would interject whenever he became bored to tears by the conversation with our driver or from staring at the procession of private, public and business vehicles.

We had reserved rooms at the same hotel as on our last visit here. I was looking forward to the week ahead here from the business perspective but more truthfully, from knowing that Suchada had a few days free on her roster that coincided with our stay.

The familiar sail shape of the unique and famous 7-start hotel, the Burj Al Arab, could be seen at a distant, vaguely discernable through the veil of dust now prevalent in Dubai.

Barry pointed out the hotel then he turned to Suchada, saying:

"I wonder if they ever have fog here. In London we have our smog, our disgusting mix of smoke and fog I supposed Dubai would have *dog"* he joked

"*Dog:* you've lost me Barry." Suchada confessed, she smiled because we laughed but she was unable to fully understand the merriment. Neither was the driver judging by the uncertainty of his laugh.

"Dog, dust and fog luv" Barry explained. This time Suchada laughed with understanding but our driver was further confused.

"Fog love?" he asked

"Yes, fog love, Hassan" Barry said, without an attempt to further clarify.

"Ah ok! Fog love, yes, funny you are, Mr. Barry" said the driver. They must have exchanged names at some stage during their conversation at the front.

"Oh just call me Barry, how do you say 'hello' in Arabic then Hassan?" Barry inquired.

"Salam-a-le-kum" Hassan carefully enounced.

"Ah yeah I know that one, what about 'thank you'. How do you say that?" Barry continued enthused.

"You can say 'shu-kran', you try it" said Hassan the teacher. I was glad not to be sitting in front of Barry at this stage as his attempt at enunciating the second part of that word was too 'fluid' for my liking as he taxed his throat beyond it's natural limits to get the pronunciation right. The driver deftly wiped off Barry's saliva from his right ear encouragingly saying:

"Yes, yes, correct. Good. Your Arabic is good Barry" His new pupil beamed at the praise.

As we pulled in to the car park of the hotel and headed for the drop-off point it felt good to return here. Two doormen opened the rear passenger doors. I saw Barry about to grumble when his door was also opened by the doorman on his side of the car.

"Shu-ka-ran" said Barry to Hassan as we paid our fare.

"Shukran, habibi. Ma-salama" replied Hassan.

And Barry couldn't leave it at that.

"What does all that mean then?" he asked his new friend.

"Thank you my friend and goodbye" Hassan the patient teacher explained.

He pulled his taxi away with a wave to us as we stepped through the rotating doors and entered the buzzy foyer of the hotel. This time the piano that magically appeared in the middle of water to the left side of the very spacious reception was being played. At first glance it was not apparent how she, the pianist reached the piano since it stood on a tiny stage surrounded by water up to just below the base of the stage.

"Perhaps she's a mermaid" Suchada quipped, noticing my quizzical glance at the pianist.

She then went to sit down, not too far from the reception area to wait for us to finish checking in.

Once done, I invited her to join me upstairs while I settled my luggage in the room. As I had half-expected, she declined saying she would wait for me in the foyer.

"Are you sure?" I asked

"Yes of course, don't worry, I won't be kidnapped. Go on, I'll be fine" she replied

"Ok, if you're sure. I won't be long. I'll just dump my stuff and freshen up a bit then I'll be right down. See you shortly"

I admired her discretion. She was lovely, I thought. Even though we'd talked a lot online since that wonderful adventure on the dunes and the night camp of the desert safari, she wasn't making it at all easy for me. I liked that very much.

Barry was waiting for me at the elevator. Our rooms were on different floors and I got out of the elevator first. We agreed to meet for dinner so that left me free to have lunch with Suchada as it was only 11:30am almost.

***

I felt guilty leaving her sitting alone downstairs so I unpacked as quickly as I could and showered even faster. The phone rang as I was stepping out of the shower. My immediate thoughts were 'oh, no, not them again'.

Sure enough, it was a girl, a different girl this time but playing the same old game. Then I had a mischievous thought. I replaced the phone once I'd finished and smiled a smile of satisfaction to my reflection in the floor-to-ceiling mirror.

I'd just finished dressing and was stepping out of the room when the phone ran again. It was Barry as I had expected.

"Tobi you tosser; I'll get you later mate!" he said, laughing.

"Don't tell me you didn't like the girl I sent you, compliments of the house" I said. "Revenge is sweet. Revenge is mine! Have fun mate, I'm off. I'll let you know if Suchada has an ugly sister for you"

"Yeah, yeah, I'll be waiting, but I'll go and soak up on some sun by the pool. I'll be brown like you in no time. Enjoy yourself!"

He hung up and a moment I'd been waiting for, arrived. The

elevator doors opened and I entered. In no time it was two floors away from the ground level. Once again I was engrossed in the awesome view through the elevator's glass walls. The shimmer of the sea was a fresh reminder that I was in a land of sun, sand, sea and sky of blue!

She smiled and looked pleased to see me back but not half as much as I was to see her and be with her knowing we had practically the whole day together. We would be alone; no Barry with us this time. She was all mine and we both anticipated a good time together. We had talked about our first real date many times on the net and now, here we were. We made our way through the milling mix of tourists in the lobby. Some just checking in and others walked surreptitiously around in their beach-wear with large beach towels wrapped around their waist. Although skimpy beach-wear was frowned upon by the hotel, yet they were obviously successful in attracting holiday makers as the vast bulk of their patronage. They mingled with business men in their Western suits and Arabic national costumes. It was a riot of colours that was a feast for the eyes.

The doormen were busy as cars pulled up and pulled away like clockwork, even the occasional coach pulled in with a load of predominantly European guests for the hotel.

A friendly doorman helped us to call a taxi away from the rank. I tipped him and we sat in the back, closely. The taxi rolled away from the hotel, past Wild Wadi Water Park adjacent to the hotel and turned around at the roundabout giving us a perfectly clear and close view of the magnificent Burj Al Arab hotel.

"It's lovely isn't it?" Suchada commented. "Can you see the helipad at the top edge? It's no longer used for helicopter landings apparently. It seems there was a vibration problem so for safety reasons they stopped using it as a helipad. They turned it into a tennis court now"

"That's a tennis court up there?" I exclaimed, truly surprised.

"Yes, can you believe that?" She replied

"Difficult to believe anyone's crazy enough to even go up there to play tennis in the first place, any balls that looked even close to going over the edge would just have to keep going. Unless the player thinks he can grow wings on the way down to catching it!" We laughed and Suchada squeezed my hand reminding me that not more than two weeks ago, Carlene had done exactly the same, with exactly the same effect of causing my heart to beat significantly faster.

14

We arrived at a Sushi bar set in a large modern mall called Bur Juman at the centre of one of the disparate hearts of Dubai.

I asked Suchada as we sat down on high stools set around the oval shaped bar where we could watch the chefs working in the middle. "This is a British Sushi bar chain isn't it? We have one like this in Piccadilly Circus in London and I remember reading something there about it being British"

"Well I'm not sure but we can ask"

"Not important" I said. "Tell you what though, the food looks great here, more fresh perhaps" I observed.

"So your father's Japanese. Does that mean you're an expert on Japanese cuisine and I'm in good hands?!"

"You must be joking; I hardly know the Japanese side of me." She replied.

"Oh, really, what do you mean, if it's not too private to discuss."

"No it's ok; well it is personal but that's ok." She paused; caught in a moment of what I assumed was long-distance mental time travel.

"Dad lives and works in Japan. A city called Kyoto. It's only since I started working with the airline that I started to get closer to him. We have regular flights to Japan and since I speak Thai and Japanese as well as English, I get a lot of Asian flights so I can see him. But of course not for long due to the flight operations so maybe a day or sometimes he just drops by the hotel when I'm in town. He and mum often send things to each other via me. He's re-married now but I know he still loves my mother a lot and she is still in love with him." She explained as she sub-consciously picked out a dish off the bar carousel which rolled the tasty dishes temptingly under the nose of the diners.

She opened it and asked me to try it, assuring me that I would like the California Maki roll. She then took another dish for herself. Well, they were actually bowls each with its base painted a specific colour denoting the price of the portion in it.

"Was your father living in Thailand at one time?" I asked her.

"Yes, when he was married to mum. They met when dad went to work in Thailand. He was transferred there by the company he worked for in Japan. He left Thailand when I was just over 5 years old. His company was his life. I think it's typical for his generation of Japanese so when he was asked to return to Japan, he did. Mum had a successful jewelry business and still does. They thought they could manage the distance but in the end he met and married a Japanese woman after seeking mum's divorce approval. She understood and accepted the inevitable and wanted only his love which he's never stopped giving. That's it, in a nutshell" She said. She was close to shedding a tear, I could feel it.

"Thank you for sharing it with me dear. Your mum and dad sound like great people. I hope I'll get a chance to meet them both. I mean, look at you. Look at what they produced!" I joked and put my arm across her shoulder to hug her momentarily.

"You're sweet Tobi"

"Yes well that must mean you like sweet tasting chocolate, all the way to the centre then." I teased.

"As a matter of fact, I can't resist chocolate even though I know it's not good for me." She teased back.

"Oh, oh, wrong answer! What's *that* supposed to mean?!"

"Ok, tell me the story of your chocolate factory then maybe I'll decide later just how big a bite of you I should take!"

I liked her sense of humour, so in tune with mine. I told her my story. I started from my early years in Lagos, my chocolate factory. I even told her about my ancestor Scipio Vaughan – to use his slavery name. In those dark days of rampant human slavery, he had been kidnapped by slavers as a very young man and taken to South

Carolina to work in the fields there. He became a skilled craftsman and was able to receive earnings for this side job. He eventually saved enough to buy his freedom and married a Cherokee woman with whom he had 13 children. Two of the children, brothers became very successful merchants and traveled back to Africa to settle very successfully in Liberia and Nigeria. And I brought her right back to the point of when she and I met.

"Wow, that's quite a story! And how is she now?" She asked, referring to Carlene.

"She's separated still and plans to arrange for her daughter to be with her as soon as possible in England."

"You must be so happy to be finally together with her again." She said. That innocent, seemingly supportive statement was a trap. Women have caught me out with that before. I answer to the positive and I lose them, answer the other way and they feel they still have a fighting chance. I couldn't lie to Suchada even though I was starting to like her ever so much.

"Yes, I am actually"

"That's amazing really. You were so passionate about finding her, weren't you?" She said, generously, although it must hurt her a little because I know she was also having stronger feelings for me. She didn't have to say it. Anyone sitting at the bar, watching us could tell we were close.

***

At the later part of spring, heading for summer, Dubai is not exactly the kind of place one would wonder around outside in the middle of the day. That is of course unless singeing the hair and skin was one's way of having fun. At 40 degrees plus only the proverbial mad dogs and English men would be out. Yet; as our taxi drove us back to the Mall of Emirates, another massive indoor shopping and everything else complex, we saw hundreds of south Asian looking construction workers laboring in the searing heat. The show must go on regarding Dubai's head-long lurch towards modernity. It's easy to criticize this policy to surge ahead regardless of the cost to human labour comfort. But as Khalifah, our host here in Dubai had inferred, the labourers get a salary that presumably makes it worth their while to be here, helping their family at home. I am personally not totally convinced by such an argument however.

The first striking image for me was the huge, tubular metal-clad ski track that jutted out from the mall's building at about 45 degrees. Rising well above the stylish mock, period design of the mall, the Dubai Ski Slope stood out from a long way off. Sporting artificial snow and ice, it was a popular attraction. From the interior of the mall, shoppers and diners could observe the fun on the ski slope and the snowy base through an enormous glass wall that separated the mall from the slope.

We had come to the complex to watch a movie. Suchada had suggested we needn't plan the movie to see, rather, just turn up and check what took our fancy at the point of arrival. Which was fine with me as that was often how I discovered good movies that I ordinarily would have avoided at all cost, some animated ones included. We settled for a romantic drama. Armed with enough snack supplies to survive any movie, we entered the theatre and were politely guided to our seats by a Filipino usher. Unlike the hubbub of the mall outside, the theatre itself was relatively tranquil with very few people inside. We sat high up in the rows of seats where we had a row to ourselves. With pleasant surprise, I found the armrest between our seats could be lifted and stowed unobtrusively all the way back; level with the backrest. Which I did and eased my arm around Suchada's shoulders despite the ambience of foreboding one starts to sense when in a highly religious nation. But somehow, Dubai seemed to surreptitiously whisper; 'it's ok as long as you don't insult our sensibilities and you conduct yourself respectably'. Every so often, when the movie released me from its grip, my mind wondered.

It was during these moments that I came to a decision. I wanted to be with both Carlene and Suchada but now I knew who I must actually choose. It became clear to me as we sat there in the dark, close and as my mind drifted to thoughts of the girl I had been unable to forget.

***

Carlene was not able to meet me at the airport as she had promised and as I had looked forward to. There had been a last minute change to her roster. She had called to tell me the day before Barry and I left Dubai. She also mentioned that she had good news to share with me and would tell me when we meet for dinner on the day I arrive. I was intrigued and told her I too had good news to tell her.

Barry and I took separate taxis as we lived in different parts of London.

We had arrived quite early in the morning but I decided against going to the office. I wanted time to think and gather the courage needed to break the heart of someone I loved deeply.

15

I met Carlene in Swiss Cottage in the North West part of London that evening; ironically at a Thai restaurant she had suggested. We both shared a love for Thai cuisine.

I arrived about fifteen minutes late having taken a wrong turn and then having parking problems. How was I going to do this? I asked myself. Carlene was radiant and I told her so.

"Hi darling, so good to see you again, you look great!" I said as I hugged her. I felt like Brutus hugging Caesar the moment before the dagger did its wicked work. But to be fair to myself, this was a totally different situation for a start, there was no deceit involved, no sabotage plotted. Just a man played as a pawn in the game of the gods. But I had a responsibility to both Carlene and Suchada to make a decision.

I remembered that once again, Suchada had turned down my invitation to come up to my room at the hotel in Dubai. After the movie we had decided to go back to my hotel for a swim and relaxation by the pool. As it had been a spur of the moment decision, we had to go back to her apartment to fetch her swimming gear. On arrival at the hotel it was then, my turn to change to swim wear. It seemed logical, even polite to invite her up to change as well. Although neither of these were my real motives but the truth was, I desired her beyond explanation.

She waited for me again in the lobby so I had zoomed up and changed Superman style but unlike him, I usually kept my underwear where it belonged, under.

Suchada had changed in the poolside changing rooms, and was

now sitting in the lobby with a beautiful sarong around her waist and a T-shirt top which was only half finished as all her flat tummy was revealed. 'Oh lord, am I in trouble' I thought.

At the pool, actually there were four of them, we looked for Barry but he was nowhere to be found, that was ok as I had feared the possibility of his crass comments on seeing Suchada like this.

It was that evening that we spent our first night together since the night in Thailand when I learned of my father's passing away.

As we sat watching an old movie in my hotel room after our swim, she told me she was developing very strong feelings for me but that she understood that I had someone I loved deeply already in my heart. She confessed she did not know how to deal with it. That was when I finally told her I was falling in love with her.

We planned to spend a two-week holiday in Thailand the following month.

I snapped sharply out of my daydream as Carlene addressed me.

"So come on, tell me, how was your trip?" she asked.

"Oh it was a success! We pulled off an amazing promotional launch for Barclays and they seemed happy with the initial results." I answered.

"Wonderful! I'm glad your trip went well. How about the rest of the trip, Dubai itself and all that" She continued.

"Are you ready to order now madam?" the smiling waitress asked Carlene who had been to the restaurant a few times before with her colleagues.

We placed our order and I requested my favourite, the Thai fried rice, Khao Phad Khai and I asked for the shrimp cakes for starters. Carlene favoured the world famous and deliciously spicy Tom Yum Khung shrimp soup.

Throughout the meal, my mind was a complete mess. The decision I thought I had made dissolved into discredit in the presence of Carlene. I hesitated to tell her anything further about the time I spent in Dubai on this last occasion for fear of revealing anything that might clue her in to what I had been up to with Suchada. Then again, I reminded myself that there was no obligation on me. I was still single, unaccounted for, unclaimed. Legally speaking, she was still married and she now has a child for another man. So who's to say she won't just get up one day, anytime soon perhaps and pick up her past life again? At this moment, sitting with her, all that argumentation meant nothing and I pushed it all as far away as I could in my mind.

"I can't wait any longer, what's your good news Su?" I asked; then I noticed my stupid gaff! I had used Suchada's nickname to address Carlene! She must have caught it I thought, but she answered as if nothing untoward had been uttered. Under the table, I crossed my fingers and hoped I'd been lucky.

"I've heard from my parents-in-law that they would be able to arrange for Megan to come and spend her summer vacation with me here!"

"That's brilliant! Congratulations!" I said, happy that Carlene would at last get to be with her daughter again, having been separated from her for well over a year now.

"Thank you. She'll be here in about six weeks or so. I'm really excited, I can't wait to see her and for her to meet you!" She said excitedly. I felt more than a twinge of guilt at these words from her. It all just made my task harder, more impossible if there is such situation.

"How long will she be able to stay with you?" I asked her.

"Almost two months. It seems short already but I'm still not really ready to have her live here yet. I have to think it through very well as you can imagine."

"Yes I know what you mean. Kids need stability don't they plus she would have made a lot of friends over there I imagine. That's a lot to make her give up to come and live in a totally new country." I said, sympathizing with her.

"Right; and they need continuity, I'm afraid my separation from her father isn't helping in that regard. Bob sees her of course and I think it's been a good thing to have Megan stay with her grandparents so they've been able to offer continuity. Bob has moved back up to Dakota to be with his beloved Satana so at least the good thing is he can be in the city with Megan and her grandparents."

"What do you think you want to do about your separation

status?" I asked not daring to anticipate a positive answer since that would only throw my mind into further turmoil.

"I'm not sure. I just know I have to do what's right for Megan. Leaving Bob was the right thing to do at the time. I'm sure of that. But now I'm confused about how my future could look like."

"What do you mean?" I wondered.

"Well here I am, back in England after a failed marriage to a man I loved in England and moved to the US for. I have an adorable and beautiful, fast growing daughter, that lives in a different country from me and I am only just settling myself in a new job and a new life here." She paused.

"My life is a mess right now and it's hard to see my way ahead." She continued. I was touched, deeply. The tears were not far away in her eyes, I was certain of that. I clasped her hand and squeezed gently as she sat next to me. I wanted to give her words of encouragement yet how could I, knowing what I eventually had to tell her. I felt callous. She was down and there is no way I would hurt her with words describing a decision which I was no longer so sure about. I held her hand tighter and whispered in her ear.

"How would you like to come with me to Thailand in about six weeks from now darling?" I said to her.

She pulled her head away and looked at me in surprise.

"What? Tobi don't play with me, please. Not now" She pleaded with misery still apparent in her expression.

"I'm serious. I have an invitation to attend a literary awards ceremony in Bangkok in six weeks from now. My book, your book really, has been included in a short list for one of the awards!" I told her, with a big smile.

"I would love you to be there with me, win or not." I continued. Her expression brightened so much that I was happy I had this news to rescue the situation.

"Oh, Tobi that is so wonderful; really so; amazing! Congratulations honey, I always said you were a special guy, you really deserve this and; thank you, thank you for considering taking me along."

"Carlene, who else could I think of to be with me but you."

"Suchada perhaps; or should I say: 'Su'?" She said rather than asked. She *had* noticed then. But her words were laced generously with a teasing flavor. There was no reproach at all in them.

"Sorry about that slip of the tongue. So you will come won't you? Say you will". I implored her.

"How can I not say 'yes' honey, I never want to not go anywhere with you again. I made that mistake once; I won't be a fool like that again."

16

For the second time, I was anticipating Suchada at an airport as I arrived. This time it was at Thailand's Don Muang International airport in Bangkok. This time it was much harder to pick her out of the large crowd as I went through the sliding doors that released us into this tropical paradise. Luckily and thoughtfully of her, she had sent me a message welcoming me to her country and telling me to turn left after the same doors. Either way that I looked, left or right, the cleared walkway lead to a channel created by layers upon layers of mostly Thai faces all eagerly looking for the travelers they had come to meet. As I dutifully turned left, I was greeted by calls from pretty hotel booking agents and limousine service agents all competing for the business of passengers spilling through the chomping mouth of the sliding doors. Almost like a mother seagull regurgitating the latest catch for her hungry and waiting fledglings to feed on. I stopped at the foreign exchange counter to get some Thai baht, the local currency. I peered expectantly at the layers of faces and she was there, pretty as ever and holding a bouquet that dared to compete with Suchada's beauty.

With the bouquet clenched between her palms, she gave me the Thai traditional greeting, the *Wai.* It's such a graceful expression of warmth and welcome or goodbye and when it's such a beauty as Suchada extending this greeting form, it's all the more enchanting. I returned the *Wai* as best as I could but could still not resist the temptation of physical contact. I hugged her and gave a kiss on her cheek being wary not to go against the local customs, Suchada kissed me back, right smack on the lips. Well that clears one particular point of uncertainty, I thought. I got such a buzz just as I did the first time I visited Thailand. It seems so unhindered yet with unspoken guidelines for having fun without encroaching on others. Suchada took my hand and we walked towards the airport exit towards the taxi rank outside but once again we were approached by limousine agents. I wanted our holiday to get off on a luxurious start so I hired a Mercedes C-Series chauffeured car to take us to the hotel.

"Hi honey! It's great to see you again. You stole the show back there at the airport, you look amazing!" I told her as we sat closely at the back of the car and our driver negotiated his way out of the airport and into the infamous, dense traffic of Bangkok.

"Thank you and welcome again to my country!" she said "I'm so excited that we can spend this time together and here. I'm really looking forward to showing you around as much as we can during our vacation"

"Me too, come on tell me some of the ideas you have for us, I'm your puppet to do what you want with for the next two weeks!" I asked eagerly.

"Hmm ok but first, how was your flight?"

"The food was great and the in-flight entertainment of your company was impressive as per the last time I used them. I replied, "I did get stuck in a row of seats with a young family where the two babies took turns to test the bursting point of my eardrums!" I continued; the memory still fresh in my ears. "Every now and then they started off a crescendo of other nearby babies crying; then the plane section enjoyed an operatic performance that came free with the flight ticket." We laughed out.

"Well that was just a one-off occasion for you but I need to face that every day at the 'office' but I like babies, so cute and adorable." Suchada said. "I don't envy the parents having to keep them entertained somehow. Especially on the longer flights, of course we're trained to help as much as we can and we do."

"Your 'office' at 35,000 feet you mean?" I asked, amused by her humour. "Ok so what's the plan? Oh and thanks for booking the hotel by the way"

"You're welcome. Let's get to the hotel and freshen up first then we go for lunch at the seafood restaurant you like in Petchburi Road."

"Ah yeah I remember. The one opposite the hotel I stayed in last time, the Amari Watergate hotel." I said, recollecting the tasty fresh crab that I had picked out from the glass tank at the restaurant.

"Yep, that's the one, I can't remember its name though but we can also do some shopping at the street stands on the other side of the road from there and at Central World Plaza mall just around the corner from there too." Suchada said.

"How long do you think we should spend in Bangkok, enough to get a flavor of it?" I asked her.

"Hmm not sure honey it depends on what you want to do and see. But I guess four days should be ok."

"What's there to see that you think would be interesting?"

"Well there's Wat Phra Kaew, that's the most famous royal palace complex in Bangkok and I suppose in Thailand. It's beautiful" She informed.

"Then that's a must!" I said enthused.

"Yes; the national museum is close-by too. We can also go to snake farm, do a day trip to crocodile farm and the floating market. These are outside of Bangkok but day trips away."

"So you mean we can use our hotel in Bangkok as a base and do day trips to these places?" I asked her.

"Yes, exactly; what do you think?"

"Yeah I'll go with that, god I'm starving. I love Thai food but maybe you're the tastiest of all. I'll start with you!" I joked, leaning towards her neck with a faked bite.

"Only if you're ready for food poisoning" she replied, leaning away from my bite. We glided to a halt at the front of the 5-star Grand Hyatt Erewan hotel in the heart of an exclusive shopping area of Bangkok. The hotel design and structure was truly grand and splendid and was perfectly located for the BTS overhead train system as well as the new underground metro train service. Top malls and shops were within easy walking distance although the heat dared you to try walking too far at a single stretch.

Checking in was smooth and we got a free upgrade to a junior suite just by pure luck. Although the view of the area was great, we didn't plan to spend too much time in the room admiring it. As with the initial room Suchada had booked, our suite had twin beds. She couldn't have made her point more clearly but I was getting used to it and to be honest, it just made me desire her more. She's clearly a kind of girl that would not be easily distracted from our relationship by other men. That's the kind of girl to introduce to a mother.

"Before we leave the hotel we can book our first trip outside of Bangkok. They have a good tour agency in-house in the lobby." Suchada suggested as she unpacked for me first then started on her own luggage.

***

We emerged into the bright mid-afternoon sun of Bangkok and entered a taxi as a hotel doorman opened the car door for us. We were heading for a late lunch at the seafood restaurant in Petchburi Road. I looked out of the taxi at the numerous, gaily coloured and covered tri-bikes that buzzed around the choked traffic.

"Those look like fun to try" I remarked.

"Yes, they're called Tuk-Tuks. They're very popular with tourists but they're used a lot by the local too. Cheap and they can get around when the taxis get stuck in traffic" Suchada informed.

"Let's try one later ok?" I said enthused.

"Of course but get ready for noise and pollution!" Suchada replied as she snuggled so closely.

It was the beginning of a perfect two weeks vacation with Suchada in Thailand.

17

I maneuvered my way through London's evening traffic, heading towards the M25 motorway. Infamously also known as the biggest car park in the country. I remember my brother, Deji, had once called me on his mobile saying he was stuck in the traffic at a section of the circular motorway. He said he was quite happily walking around amongst the stationary cars that jammed all the lanes; making and receiving his business phone calls. The motorway, they dared not call it an express way, had been built around London to help ease the traffic the old city continuously traded with the rest of the nation. The number of lanes had been expanded every now and then and more cars and lorries just turn up from seemingly nowhere.

Just as with personal computers, as soon as Intel produce more powerful and faster processor chips for computers, Microsoft seem to always come out with more power hungry software to gobble up the processor power and clog up the computer. Ergo the endless chain of supply and demand.

I was on my way to see Su, she had arrived on a 'layover' flight and had a night free. She was staying at a hotel near Gatwick Airport and masochistically, I had decided to go all the way there to pick her up and go out for a night in town, London town that is. But luckily for me, she had agreed to spend the night at my place so I would not have to drive her back so late at night. As it turned out, I ended up staying at her hotel and having a rather comfortable drive back the next morning. We decided to just 'hang out' at a local pub and to have a chat then dinner at the restaurant in the hotel. She didn't want to be too tired on the return flight the next day and as she didn't want me to drive back to London to late either, I ended up staying with her that night. The evening had been going very well until she brought up a subject I hadn't considered and worse, hadn't considered could have threatened my relationship with her.

***

As we sat in the bed that night with only the flickering light of the television to illuminate the room, she had again rejected my amorously lecherous approach. Until now all we had ever done was to kiss and cuddle despite my unashamedly passionate attempts in Dubai earlier. I was impressed and depressed simultaneously, with her resolute manner. Her deep feelings for me were unhidden as were mine for her but from somewhere deep in her personality, upbringing or culture or a mix of these, she always appeared to find the strength to control our sensual situations.

But tonight was different. She was tense. She sat up in the bed propping her back on the headboard with two pillows stuffed between.

"Tobi, I talked with both my parents about us, about you. About how we met, about the way we feel for each other. I told them of my love for you. Yes Tobi, I do love you." At her words, her protestation of love for me, my heart leapt in a staccato fashion.

"I love you too Su. More and more each time we meet." My sixth sense told me there was a 'but' fast approaching. Then it arrived. Her next words were spoken through a veil of tears that I knew were there only because of the quality of sadness in her voice. Her heart had been broken by the two people she loved and looked up to most in her life.

"Mum was furious." She sobbed. "Dad didn't even want to discuss it further as soon as I told them who you were, where you came from; that you are a black guy. I hate my parents Tobi. After all those years they taught me about love and compassion and judging people on an individual bases, on their merit and without prejudice. Now they react like this when I finally find someone I care for and love as I do you." As she said this, my emotions were mixed, churning in a blend of opposing sensations. I was elated at knowing Suchada loved me and did so enough to tell her parents. I realized this was not easy for her. After all she comes from a conservative Asian background where even breathing a word about a love or possible suitor had to be well considered in advance of such an announcement. Her mother for one was considered of high-society in the Bangkok community.

But her revelation had cost her dearly and I sympathized with her. On the other side, I felt rage and indignation. I was angered at the overt racial discrimination which had driven her parents to reject us, to reject me for being of a different race. A race, apparently, not considered worthy of a relationship, certainly not of one based on mutual love, with their daughter. My mind screamed the words I know Suchada also wanted to say. Had they forgotten that they had themselves formed a taboo relationship and that their lovely daughter was a product of such a mix?

"Both my parents had faced immense pressure from their families not to be together when they were told I was on the way and that they wanted to get married." She said with frustration. She was completely devastated. It was then I realized how tender her feelings were for me, how she must have battled with her intuition and knowing a clash was ahead with her parents. Yet she had faced them with hopes of being wrong, that they would understand and accept whatever man made their only daughter happy. She had lost. They had combined to break her heart and hopes. My protective instinct made me experience a fuming rush of anger at her parents; how dare they hurt her like this?!

I pulled her close to my chest and reached to the side-able for the box of tissues. I took out a wad of the soft tissues and dabbed at the tracks of her tears. I kissed her gently on her forehead, brushing her long, thick black hair with my finger tips. She was motionless and cried softly until I kissed her lips and she responded. We were united in our sense of misery and of the injustice dished out to us by a world that saw through eyes oversensitive to colour and creed. I wanted to console her and let her know how much I cared for her. I too, craved comforting. We found our momentary peace in the sweet love that we made that night.

***

On the drive back to London the next morning, I realized the question of whether my mother would accept Suchada had never been discussed. It didn't need to be. Judging from the ease and warmth with which Carlene had been taken in to our family, I saw no likelihood of hesitation on the part of my mother at the introduction of Suchada to her. But now I could not contemplate taking my mother through the heartbreak of introducing her to Suchada. It was with a major effort that I had managed to eventually tell her that Rosemary and I were no longer together. She had been incredulous as she could not fault Rosemary at all and is in normal contact with her and invites her home for meals and chit chat as per usual. I saw no reason to discourage her since Rosemary and I remained good friends. And I had gotten over our breakup with the help of discovering Suchada and the finding of Carlene again. Mum had, as had dad, been over the moon about Carlene yet I also had been forced to inform them that I had lost her. That was my own doing or undoing depending on how you looked at it. Now I know I definitely could not hurt or disillusion my mother again by dangling Suchada in front of her knowing her family had rejected me and worse, rejected our race.

Suchada had insisted that she would bend her parents' mind to her will, and that we would be left to form our relationship. My feeling was different; I wanted to give her a chance to reach her parents' hearts, I really did. It would have been to no avail, I was sure of that. Their anti-black sensitivities would be deep-rooted, based on fears and stereotypical negativity re-enforced daily in the media and multiplied by their society's sense of value. It would be an uphill battle that would dog us through our lives.

All this said, I wanted, just as did Suchada to take them all on. To prove we would work. I was however not willing to let her pay the high price of long lasting discord with her parents, her family, her society. But especially, not with her parents; her relationship with them was far too precious.

As we made love last night, the one and only night, it was as if in defiance of her parents' clear blindness. To show there were some things that even they could not stop, could not block or intrude upon. In the intimate cover of our last night alone together we had triumphed and won a magnificent battle by mutual expression of our love. The reality of the cold light of day told the full story however. The victory of the war belonged to Suchada's parents. They had connived and persuaded her to resign from her job and return to Thailand from where she would then be sent to Japan to study her MBA as preparation for her taking over the family's growing international business.

***

Two months later I walked hand in hand with Carlene in Hyde Park, under the willow trees again. I thought of how the literary awards ceremony in Bangkok had gone very well. 'Carlene', the book had won a prize for the best first novel and Carlene, my one and only everlasting love had been beside me on stage to receive the award. We had then spent a wonderful week touring the beautiful islands of southern Thailand before returning home to England. We promised ourselves to return to Thailand soon.

We walked until we reached the pond. We were totally engrossed in ourselves and our love although Carlene kept a watchful parental eye on the beautiful little girl that played happily with the squirrels ahead of us. At our first day of meeting, Megan had captivated me with her charm and spirit and our world was now complete except for one thing. Although we'd still have to wait a little longer, our villa alone on the cliff was not so far away now thanks to 'Carlene', the book.

~End~

www.ingramcontent.com/pod-product-compliance
Ingram Content Group UK Ltd.
Pitfield, Milton Keynes, MK11 3LW, UK
UKHW020135250726
13967UKWH00002B/659